The Fifth Chamber

By

Jennifer Dillow

Cover Art: J.C. Dillow

ISBN 978-0-9966154-1-9

First Edition

There are worlds we have yet to explore. There is a vast and endless expanse of wilderness that awaits less than two steps from our doorway.

- Jeffrey C. Dillow

ADVENTURES IN HIGH FANTASY

CONTENTS

CHAPTER 1

Monsters

I sit down on the chilly floor in the corner of my room, and scrunch into the shadows of the early morning trying my best to disappear. Clutching my talisman, I press my back up against the wall hoping it will somehow consume me. As if the dark is safer.

It's so silly. And yet here I am.

All that I have left of my parents is this talisman around my neck and a promise of war. A parting gift right before they sent me and my brother away. Now, I can barely remember their faces and I'm running out of time. But no matter how hard I stare at it, curse at it, bang it against the floor, nothing happens. I squeeze the talisman so hard I feel it cutting into my skin, like squeezing the life out of it can somehow save me from tonight.

Nothing can save me now.

I stare at it so intently that I forget to blink and my eyes begin to water. The intricate gold work on the talisman appears to blend

1

into its silvery body and I can no longer make out its circular shape. Accepting defeat, I pry my fingers one by one from the vice-like grip they've formed and cup the delicate-looking trinket in the palm of my throbbing hand. My talisman disorder is definitely in full force this morning.

Classes begin today. It's not exactly the birthday present that I was hoping for, and the idea of heading back to school on a day like today seems ridiculous. I see no point to bother with high school now. My guardians disagree. They assure me that blending in with the people of this realm will help us remain hidden from those who would hunt us. Deception is vital.

Except I know deep down that school is not what's bothering me. Today is significant for another reason, not just because it's my sweet sixteen and the threat of school is lingering in the air.

I've always known that this day was coming. I tried to block it out, and yet it still managed to find its way to me, tracking me day by day like a stealthy fox, creeping up behind me when I wasn't looking. I didn't stand a chance. This is the day I'll be called back to my people to begin my training for war. The day of The Summoning has arrived. And tonight, after school, I will be summoned to the realm from which I came so it all can begin. From here on, my nights will be filled with weapons and violence and blood. My brother and guardians will remain here in this non-magical world when I leave them to train, quietly hiding. Blending.

I force my eyes away from my talisman and groggily turn towards the nightstand. The demonic red lights from the clock reveal the disturbing truth. It's 3:30 in the morning. I compel myself up off of the floor and tuck the talisman inside of my white t-shirt. I pull on a pair of jeans, boots, and my favorite brown leather jacket – the weathered looking one with little tears near the pockets – and head downstairs. I try to move as quietly as possible so I don't wake anyone else. I want the peacefulness that comes with morning to last as long as possible.

I manage to make it down the creaky stairs without making too much noise. This is quite an accomplishment considering the unforgiving nature of our old colonial when it comes to sound absorption. Just as I go to reach for the door handle, I hear our white husky, Sasha, make a whimpering sound, demanding my attention. She looks up at me with her frosty blue eyes, but it's too early in the morning for it to have the desired effect. I tell her to hush and go cuddle with my twelve-year old brother, Pax, who's always been her favorite. I hope having Sasha around will help my brother cope when I'm gone.

I open up the door and walk outside into the woods behind our house. It's the beginning of September and the air has just a hint of fall in it. The morning dew on the leaves makes the forest glisten as the sun starts peeking through the trees. I keep walking until I reach the spot where the old gnarled-looking oak grows. My socks are soaked from the condensation that has seeped through my worn-out boots. "This is where it will happen," I mutter, as I lean my back against the massive tree and slump down to the ground. My talisman disorder kicks in and I start absentmindedly fiddling with it as per normal procedure when I need comfort.

It's been weeks since I had a good night's sleep, since I've had a clear head. I'm haunted by incessant nightmares and thoughts of war, and I'm starting to think that I'll never see another peaceful night. No matter what I do, I can't stop my mind from racing. Visions of Western corpses dance around in my head. Lines of chained prisoners fill my brain. Is this my future? If the stories are true then it very well could be. I don't see how my going back there is going to make any difference. I didn't choose to be part of the Bravura, but I guess sometimes you just don't have a choice.

I try to clear my mind, focusing on the forest noises. The forest has always had a calming effect on me. I hear the birds beginning their morning melodies. A tiny symphony of crickets plays in the background. A rustle of leaves lets me know a forest creature is nearby – maybe a squirrel or a rabbit?

THUMP! I recognize the sound of an arrow piercing a nearby tree. I turn my head towards the sound and see a rabbit pinned to a tree trunk.

"Kenlin?" I ask, tentatively.

"What are you doing up so early?" comes a deep voice from behind me.

"Right back at ya," I respond.

"Couldn't sleep. I figured I'd get some hunting in. Want to join me?"

"Maybe we could just train?" I suggest, hoping to avoid seeing anymore dead animals this morning.

"Good idea. Any little bit helps."

I stand up and walk deeper into the forest towards our training site until I reach the small wooden shed that sits on the perimeter. I

open one of the creaky doors. Inside are dozens of weapons for my choosing. I grab a knife and a crossbow. Shoving the knife down my boot, I turn confidently towards Kenlin.

"Let's see what you can do," he says.

All around, there are targets arranged at varying distances. Little straw dummies with little tin can hearts. I have to strain my eyes to see them in the dim light. I take aim at a dummy about fifty yards away, wedged in between two large trees. There is little room for error. The morning light reflects off the tin can like a tiny beacon in the distance. I draw the string until it is locked, and I make sure that the bolt is seated in place. Squeezing the trigger gently, with control, I release the bolt. The dummy gets it straight through the tin can.

"Good. Now that one," Kenlin says, pointing farther into the forest.

I smile, ready for the challenge. To show just how ready I am, I drop my crossbow, dive to the ground, and somersault into a crouched position before whipping the dagger through the air.

I miss.

"If I've told you once, I've told you a hundred times, Arden. When you throw a knife or shoot an arrow, it will travel in a straight line. You'll do better to stay on your feet and aim straight."

"Sorry. I know. I'll keep it simple."

"Just stick to what you know and you'll be fine. I have faith in you."

"Swords?" I ask, wanting to change the subject.

"Sure," he says and pulls two gleaming blades from the shed. "Move fast!" he shouts, tossing the blade at me.

I whip my head up and pluck the sword from the air by the hilt. He lunges at me. Too obvious. I easily deflect his blade and move aside. He takes another exaggerated swing. I have plenty of time to dodge it.

"You afraid I might break?" I ask.

"Just want to make sure you don't get injured before your big day."

"I'm insulted, Kenlin. Where's your faith now?"

I lunge as if I'm about to strike him from one angle and then spin quickly around to attack him from the other side. I have to stop myself when I see that I'm about to slice through his back. He isn't even paying attention to me. He's staring off into the woods.

"Hellooo!" I say, a little agitated.

"Find cover! Now!" he whispers.

I run to the shed and slam the door shut. Through a crack in the doors, I can see that Kenlin has disappeared. He must be hiding. When Kenlin gives a command, I listen. It's his job to protect me. But what is he protecting me from now? I look out and see what he was staring at. Out of the woods, slowly creeping along the ground is a dense white fog. It's coming towards us. It seems…unnatural. It's too thick and it moves too quickly. I feel a pain in my gut as it gets closer, rolling past the trees. My heart begins to race and my chest feels hot.

The fog gathers near the spot where I dropped my crossbow, forming a thick white cloud. The cloud begins to change shape. One opaque paw steps forward, then another. Are those red eyes? The constant swirling of the cloud muddles my vision and makes it hard to tell. The creature is fluid, not fully formed.

I look through the crack of the door, searching for Kenlin. The creature seems to be searching for something too. The fog flows around the training site, changing shape as it moves.

I see the top of Kenlin's arrows poking out from behind a nearby rock. The fog moves ever closer to his hiding spot. Kenlin is almost discovered when I let out a gasp. The distorted shape of a wolf's head turns in my direction. Trembling, I try to control my heavy breathing. Can it see me?

As if in response, it begins moving deliberately towards the shed, taking its time all the while. I hold my breath as it gets closer. A red eye peeks through the crack and it sounds almost as if something is sniffing near the door. To my horror, fog starts seeping through the cracks. BOOM! A loud noise from the forest causes the fog to retreat. It flies towards the direction of the sound.

I remain standing in the shed, shaking, with my arms pinned to my sides. A statue frozen in fear.

The doors to the shed tear open. "Run home," Kenlin commands.

It takes me a second to get my feet to move, but once they do, I fly through the forest towards my home. Kenlin does not follow me.

I reach the back of our house and the brightness of the sun alerts me to the fact that the day is beginning. I burst through the back door into the kitchen and find Marion putting some water on the stove for her morning tea. She drops the kettle when she sees me.

"What's wrong?"

"In the woods...a creature...glowing eyes..." I say, between gasps for air.

"Where's Kenlin? Was he with you?"

"Yeah...he's still out there!"

She looks at me with her determined brown eyes. "Go get ready for school. I'll handle this."

"Who cares about school? I have to help Kenlin!"

"Kenlin knows what he's doing. If he didn't come back with you it was for a reason. He's probably trying to make sure you're safe. That's what we're here for – to protect you."

"But Marion, you don't understand. I've never seen anything like it!"

"That's enough, Arden," she says, pausing to collect herself. "You know, you're right. Kenlin does need your help. What he needs you to do is keep up appearances and act normally. You never know who is watching you and we haven't been in hiding for over ten years only to be caught now."

"Fine, but you better come get me if anything happens."

"Don't you worry about Kenlin. He can handle himself."

With a huff, I run upstairs to throw on my uniform. I'll have to hurry so I don't miss my ride to school. As fast as I can, I change my clothes, grab my school bag, and come bounding back down the stairs. I see that my boots have left a muddy trail all over the house. Marion's not going to like that. I'd apologize, but she's nowhere to be found. I almost start running back towards the woods to find Kenlin, but I know that Marion's right. If there is danger, he would want me to stay as far away as possible. I have to trust him.

I make it outside just in time to see Derek next door getting into his old, beat-up Honda. I think it used to be silver at one point, but there's so much rust covering it now that I can't be sure. He throws his books in the backseat and flashes me a big smile, motioning for me to get in. When Derek smiles it's like his whole body lights up. It's hard to feel anything but happy when I'm around him. Although today, I could use a couple of extra smiles to shake me out of this mood. I'm finding it hard to get the vision of those two blood red eyes out of my head.

"Hey! You ready for the first day?" he asks as I approach the car. "Hope you don't mind showing up to school in this piece of junk. Better than the bus though, right?"

"You know I love old Betsy here," I say, as I affectionately tap the hood of the car. I slide into the passenger seat and roll down the window to let in the breeze. I want more than anything to tell Derek about what happened to me this morning. How frightening it was. I want to tell him about the significance of today and about what's going to happen to me tonight. But I can't. He's not one of us. He's from this realm, whereas I'm just a visitor.

There's some cheesy pop song that I can't stand playing on the radio so I turn it off. I don't feel like listening to music at the moment.

"What's on your mind, AJ?" Derek asks as he glances over at me. Derek calls me AJ, which is short for my first and middle names, Arden Jacinda. *Nicknames are such a guy thing*, I think to myself.

"Not much. Just sitting here thinking about how much I'm dreading today."

Derek reaches over and musses up my hair a bit. "Don't be so worried, kiddo. School's not *that* bad. Besides, you have me," he says, and throws me another flawless grin.

"True. I don't know *what* I would do without you here annoying me all day with your perfect hair and sunny disposition," I say and give him a mocking smile in return. I always tease Derek about his dark wavy hair since it looks like he just stepped out of a magazine and my long, chestnut hair, which is usually pulled back in a ponytail, is always such a mess.

"Hey now, you know me and my hair can't help being so perfect," he says with a wink.

Staring out the window, I notice how beautiful it is outside. Our small town is surrounded by nature, pure and serene. Everywhere I look I see green trees, stretching all the way to the foothills of the imposing mountains that give our home a majestic feel. This morning's incident keeps playing over and over again in my mind. It was so unnatural that it just doesn't fit. Not in this world. That horrid beast didn't come from this beautiful place. Have the monsters finally found me?

"So how much you wanna bet Emily and Ryan get back together before the end of the day?" Derek asks, snapping me back to attention.

I let out a half-hearted laugh. "I can never keep up with those two. One day they're together and the next day they hate each other. Seems kinda pointless don't you think?"

"Yeah maybe...but not all relationships are like that. When it's right, things just progress naturally, you know? You don't have to force it."

Leave it to Derek to pull something positive out of Emily and Ryan's never-ending saga. I'm baffled that he hasn't had a girlfriend yet. So far, he's been oblivious to his growing female fan club at school. He's too busy trying to fill his transcripts with A's and loads of extracurricular activities. It's going to take a lot to get where he wants to go in life, to escape the lack of wealth that he comes from. I'm hoping he stays oblivious for at least a little while longer. I'm not ready to lose my best friend. Not yet.

We pull into the school parking lot. The school building itself is an old brick structure with tapered columns and an enormous arched doorway. It's actually quite pretty. Derek's old Honda sticks out like a sore thumb in the sea of BMWs and Mercedes before us. Even the parking lot reeks of privilege. Derek is able to attend private school because he got a scholarship, which the kids here like to remind him of occasionally. Like he could forget that.

I sling my bag over my shoulder, Derek grabs his books, and we walk up the stone pathway towards the front doors of the building, preparing to enter the social piranha pool that is St. Regis.

"What's first on the agenda, AJ?"

"History," I say with a sigh. "It's cruel and unusual punishment for so early in the morning, if you ask me."

"Sorry to hear that," he says, feigning sympathy. "I've got English with Mendenhall. Should be a breeze."

"Things don't come so easily for all of us. Maybe one day you'll understand that we mere mortals have to actually study to pass. But I *would* rather have English right now. History just puts me to sleep."

"Trust me; I study plenty. I wish you had English too. Then you could sit next to me and get me in trouble for talking like you always do."

Before I have time to craft a clever response, I'm distracted by a group of kids standing out front. I expect to see the usual "in" crowd hanging outside before the first ominous bell rings, but this time something is different. Or *someone*, I should say. There are two new kids who seem to be drawing everyone's attention. I can't get a good look at them at first, but the crowd soon parts and I catch a glimpse of a boy and a girl who look to be about my age. They're giggling and the girl is showing the other kids something on her phone. Their velvety laughs are infectious and everyone seems to be in on the joke. I catch myself staring at them a little too long – it's hard to look away. They both have shiny blonde hair and porcelain-like skin. Their faces are slim and their features are somewhat sharp, giving an edge to their look. Paired with piercing green eyes, they're unusually attractive. They look so much alike that they must be related. The girl sees me looking over and our eyes meet for just a second. I immediately feel something strange, something in my gut, almost like a slight pain. I quickly look away and hurry inside. As I pass by, I notice that my chest feels warm and I automatically grab my talisman. I have to release it immediately. It's red-hot. I begin to rip it off, but I stop as I'm about to lift it over my head. I never take off my talisman. As uncomfortable as it is to wear it at the moment, it would feel worse not to have it on. I let it drop back down, accepting the sting of the burn. My heart quickens as I start thinking about what this could mean. Maybe all that banging it on the floor did something. I start mentally preparing a list of questions to interrogate Marion with as soon as I get the chance.

History is just as bad as I had anticipated. I try to hide in the back of the room, but somehow Mr. Gerber still finds me, making me his first victim. He asks me what year the Civil War began, but I'm too distracted with memories of this morning to form a complete thought. I dumbly reply, "Umm…," staring at him blankly until he moves on to the next poor soul. So much for first impressions. Mercifully, History eventually ends, but the entire morning drags on and I find myself counting down the minutes until the lunch bell rings. I just can't concentrate on school. Not when I don't know for certain if Kenlin is alright.

I hear the bell and hurry outside to meet Derek at our bench in the courtyard behind the school. I call it "our bench" because we've been eating here together every sunny day for the past two years. We both prefer to avoid the cafeteria if we can. I see Derek across the way heading towards me – he doesn't look half bad in the navy uniforms we have to wear – they bring out his blue eyes. He plops his sturdy body down next to me and tosses over a bag of chips. "I got these for you. I figured you might need some extra munchies today."

"Thanks," I say casually, as I try not to let on how much I want to rip open the bag and devour them. My pathetic salad just doesn't compare to junk food.

"Oh yeah, I also got you something else," he says. He reaches down into his pocket and pulls out a small wrapped box. The color of the wrapping is pale yellow – my favorite. "Happy birthday. You didn't think I'd forget did you?" he asks, handing me the box.

"Actually, I kind of did," I admit, before tearing off the wrapping to see a beautifully carved wooden jewelry box with my initials, A.J., etched on the top.

"I made it myself," he says, glancing down towards his feet.

"Wow, Derek, this is *really* amazing – it must have taken you forever," I reply. I'm impressed that he has the ability to make something as gorgeous as this when I can barely make toast.

"Now you have someplace special to store that necklace you always wear," he says, reaching out to touch my talisman with his fingertips. I jerk backwards so that his fingers never quite reach it, partially out of possessiveness, but mostly for his protection. I don't know what's going on with it right now and I can't risk hurting Derek.

I can see from his face that I've hurt him.

"Thanks a lot. Seriously, this is really thoughtful," I say and gently squeeze his hand, trying to make up for my reaction. He looks up at me for a moment as our hands stay connected and there seems to be a shift in the atmosphere. We pull our hands away simultaneously and he adjusts himself in his seat, letting out a little cough. "No problem," he says, "...so, how 'bout those new kids, huh?" And just like that, the feeling is gone and we're back to normal.

"I know. What was the deal this morning? It's like people were just gravitating to them or something."

Derek swallows a bite of his peanut butter and jelly sandwich and between mouthfuls says, "Apparently, they're twins who transferred here from some public school in Jersey. You should've seen the guy in my gym class. His name is Zeke and let me tell you, that kid can shoot a basketball. I don't think I saw him miss once. I think his sister's name is Cici. I heard some guys talking about her."

I can't help but roll my eyes, my self-esteem taking a dip. It's not surprising that Cici is already the talk of the school. She looks like she doesn't even know the meaning of the term "bad hair day." "I bet," I respond with just a hint of bitterness in my voice. "I don't think any of the other girls stand a chance with her around."

Then, from the corner of my eye, deep in the surrounding bushes, I think I spot the hints of fog swirling near the ground. I look closer, but I can't be sure. Am I completely losing it? I consider grabbing Derek and making a run for it, but I hesitate just long enough for the ring of the bell to fill the air. I jump up off the bench, ready to get back inside, and I have to do a double take. I swear, just for a second, I saw two glowing red eyes staring at me from inside the bushes.

I don't know if I should run home or if I should lock myself up and throw away the key. The stress is getting to me, but I follow Marion's instructions and continue to move through the day.

Thankfully, the rest of the school day is alright. First, Gym with Ms. Hurley, who always makes her classes run so many laps at the beginning that everyone but me is sweaty and breathless within the first ten minutes. Later, I manage to forget what a derivative is in Calculus with Mr. Stein – a feat I'm not particularly proud of. By the time I'm on my way to Lit class, I'm feeling a little more like myself.

While I'm heading down the main hallway, I notice some junior guys teasing a freshman who had the unfortunate luck of being born with a cleft palate. They're hovering over the boy while he cowers at their harsh words. I see that there are three of them and quickly assess that none of them are overly large or athletic-looking. I think I could take them if it came down to it – none of these ivy-leaguers-in-training has much fight in them. Besides, they're nothing compared to what I'll have to face tonight and if there's one thing I can't stand, it's a bully. I slam my books on the ground and shove one of the boy's tormentors aside. "What do you think you're doing?"

"What are you, his mother? We're just welcoming our new freshman friend here to St. Regis," one of them replies.

"Yeah I bet. If you think *his* lip is so funny you should see what I'm gonna do to *yours* if you don't shut up."

Just then, a nearby teacher runs over and breaks us up. The freshman boy is escorted to his next class and the juniors are left to go, free and clear. I glare at them with my best *I'll get you next time* look as they walk away. I turn to go to class and I see the new kid, Zeke, across the hall at his locker, staring intently at me, almost as if he's studying me. I return his gaze and am startled at how insanely good-looking he is. I can't explain it, but something inside me is warning me to stay away, that this kind of beauty is dangerous. I find myself reluctant to look away and it takes all my effort to break eye contact.

I'm grateful when the last bell rings and the school day is finally over. One more class and I think my head would have exploded. Derek is a little late getting to his car, which allows just enough time for Zeke and Cici to walk by. Cici already seems to have made a ton of friends. I can't help but wonder how she did it. I mean, I've been here for years and my only real friends are Derek and Emily. Cici has been here for what, like two seconds, and she's already the most popular girl in school?

Before getting into their car, I catch Zeke taking one last barely-noticeable glance at me from the corner of his eye and I have to stop the smile that threatens to form on my lips. I put my head down and continue hovering by the passenger seat of Derek's car, waiting for him to arrive.

Finally, Derek saunters over, not in a rush to go home. "Sorry to keep you waiting," he says, smiling mischievously from ear to ear.

If it weren't for Kenlin, I wouldn't be in a hurry to get back today. After this morning's episode, my dread of The Summoning has taken on a new meaning. I haven't felt that kind of fear before and it makes me wonder what awaits me in this other world. Still, I can't miss an opportunity to tease Derek. "Oh please, do take your time," I reply. "It's not like it's my birthday and I have someplace to be or anything."

He rolls his eyes at me before hopping into the driver's seat.

The ride home from school today is especially hard because I know that once this car stops, I'll have to say goodbye, and not just any old *goodbye, see you tomorrow.* The Summoning is going to change everything, including me and Derek. Today could mean the end of us.

I hope he doesn't think anything when instead of our normal quick "see you later," I jump across the seat and give him a hug. I'm not much of a hugger, so he's a little surprised. To my astonishment, he doesn't flinch and instead willingly accepts my embrace and gives me a little squeeze in return. "Jeez, turning sixteen is really having an effect on you," he says, laughing a bit. His breath smells like spearmint. I hungrily breathe in the last bits of Derek I may ever get.

CHAPTER 2

The Summoning

I slide out of the car, glancing back one last time before I walk inside my front door. The house is quiet. I do a quick sweep of the first floor to see if anyone is there. I can't find anyone, so I go straight up to my bedroom to drop off my things and begin my search for my guardians. I look around at my modest room and feel a twinge of sadness. Everything about the room reminds me of what I'll be letting go of – my green and yellow baby blanket, the old concert ticket stubs and pictures from our lake trip taped to my mirror, even the chewed-up teddy bear that Sasha had her way with as a puppy. I've never been the kind of girl to get all weepy about mementos, but my emotions are a little out of whack today.

I'm not the only one who's a little off. My guardians, Marion and Kenlin, have been on edge lately, trying to prepare me as much as possible for tonight. From what they've told me, the battles between the Eastern Empire and our home in the Western Kingdoms are only getting worse. Maybe they're right to be concerned.

The worry lines are beginning to show on Marion's forehead and her normally olive complexion has turned somewhat pale as of late. She's starting to look old beyond her years. And contrary to his tough exterior, Kenlin has been unusually affectionate, which only makes it worse. I think I even saw him close to tears the other night. I hate it when guys cry.

My throat feels dry so I walk downstairs to the kitchen to pour myself some water. I find Marion sitting at the table compulsively flipping through a magazine, not even looking at the content on the pages.

"Where's Kenlin?"

"He's fine, dear. The day was quite uneventful after you left."

"And that thing in the forest?"

"Don't know. Kenlin couldn't track it. We're just going to have to keep our eyes open for any other signs."

"Signs? What kind of signs?"

"Signs that we're not alone."

I reach for my talisman and clasp it in my hand. "I don't know if this means anything, but my talisman changed temperature today – it heated up. What does it mean?"

"Are you sure?"

"I swear."

"When did it happen?"

"At school. In the morning. That's the only time I noticed it."

"Maybe the excitement from the morning made you a little flushed and it was just your body heat. Nothing to worry about."

I go to the sink to fill my glass. As I look out the window, I see Pax, Kenlin, and Sasha headed towards the house. Relief washes over me and all I can think about is that Kenlin is safe. I can feel the tears welling up in my eyes as I look out the window at my guardian and I have to fight them back. Maybe I shouldn't be so hard on Kenlin for getting a little weepy himself.

I look closer and see that Kenlin has three bloody rabbits dangling from his belt and Sasha is chewing on some sort of mutilated small animal, unrecognizable from its former self.

Pax's sandy-brown hair is starting to get a little shaggy, and he has some of his baby fat left in his cheeks. Even still, he looks like a natural warrior with arrows strapped to his back and a bow in his hand. Pax pushes open the back door to the kitchen with a loud thud – he hasn't quite mastered his own strength yet.

"Get that filthy animal out of this house!" shouts Marion from her seat.

Pax turns to Sasha, "Out! Now!" and she obediently trots out of the house, content for the moment with her kill.

Marion gets up from the kitchen table and gathers some old newspapers that were lying in a stack in the corner. She spreads out several layers of paper on the table until she's satisfied that they'll provide adequate protection. Kenlin detaches the rabbits from his belt and lays them on the newspaper with care. I run up to him and

give him a huge hug, practically knocking him into the dead animal carcasses on the table.

"Are you OK? I was so worried about you today!"

"Why wouldn't he be OK?" Pax asks.

Kenlin looks me in the eyes and says calmly, "I'm completely fine." Then he turns to Pax. "Your sister and I were out hunting this morning and we came across an animal that was a little on the wild side. Not a big deal." He looks back at me. "Isn't that right, Arden?"

"Umm…yeah," I answer, catching on that he doesn't want Pax to know about what happened. "It was…a fox."

"A fox? You were worried about Kenlin and a fox?" Pax asks.

"It was a big fox," I answer lamely.

"Right, well enough of that," Marion interrupts. "It's time to get started on dinner."

The site of the dead rabbits on the kitchen table makes me a little sick to my stomach. I'm more of a pre-packaged meal kind of girl myself. I don't mind eating meat as long as I don't know where it came from. Maybe it's hypocritical of me, but I just don't like the idea of eating anything I can picture with a face. It's too bad because I never take advantage of the woods out behind our house, which provide the perfect secluded hunting ground. Anyone who thinks hunting is just a part of nature would love it. Pax is a natural hunter. He's always out there.

"So what are we having for your last meal tonight, sis?"

"I hardly think that this is my last meal, champ," I say to Pax and give him a light jab in the arm.

"Hey, you never know, right? I mean what if those Western warriors take one look at you and decide they should just get it over with and kill you themselves?"

"That's very funny considering I can still take you in a fight. I don't care how big you're getting."

"Settle down you two," Kenlin commands. "You're both tremendous warriors," he says with just a note of sarcasm, "and as for your last meal, why, we shall be having rabbit stew of course. Complements of yours truly. Or in your case, Arden, we can make it just stew, minus the rabbit."

I decide that there's no better time than now to toughen up. "I think I'll take the rabbit tonight. I doubt they have tofu where I'm going."

Pax looks over at me with an expression of concern, "Seriously, are you nervous about tonight?"

"No way Paxy, I've got this covered – I'm one of the Bravura, remember? Besides, it's not like I'm disappearing forever. I'll be back before you know it." Hopefully, I've convinced Pax more than I've been able to convince myself. I have to laugh as I think about the name, the Bravura, and what it's supposed to represent. That I'm somehow exceptionally brave and courageous. I don't feel very brave at the moment. Marion always tells me that you don't need to feel brave to be brave. That it's in my blood and when the time comes, I'll find my bravery. If only that time wasn't coming so quickly.

"That's right, Pax. She won't be staying there until the Elders have decided that she's completed her training. She'll be back tomorrow to annoy you," Kenlin says, as he starts skinning the rabbits with his knife, their dark blood running through his fingers.

The fact that I'll return each morning after training doesn't bring me much comfort. From what I gather, where I'm headed tonight is about as safe as wearing a tin-foil hat during a lightning storm. There's no guarantee that I'll ever come back. My permanent residence in this fabulously war-torn realm doesn't really begin until I'm done training. Part of me hopes I'm a slow learner.

Kenlin finishes skinning the rabbits and tosses the leftovers out to Sasha, who gobbles them up greedily.

"Why don't we go for a ride while these two finish making dinner?" I say to Pax, motioning to Marion and Kenlin.

A love of horses is something that Pax and I both share. Sometimes we'll ride all day, losing track of the time, consumed by the horses' power. We'll come home with tired bodies, aching from the strain of holding ourselves on the saddle, but it's a good ache. The kind that lets us know we're alive. Our two golden Palominos with their ivory-colored manes are more than just our horses; they're a part of us.

When we reach the stables we find our golden friends, Gala and Nalda, chomping lazily on some hay. We greet them with carrots and Nalda nuzzles me, giving an approving whinny. Pax's horse,

Gala, lets out a snort and stomps her front leg impatiently on the ground, a sign that she's anxious to go.

"Ok, girl, let me brush you off first. Then I promise we'll get out of here," he says.

We finish saddling the horses and make our way to the riding trail we've cleared in the forest. Pax and I look at each other, "One, two, three!" We take off at a fast gallop. The trees blur by. The wind feels cold on my face, and I can't help but smile. I forget about everything for the time being. Nothing matters in this moment but the speed of my horse. Pax is a fast rider, but I'm faster. As he would say, I've had more time to practice. Horseback riding just comes naturally to us. It's part of our heritage.

Our grandfather is the Chief of the Hebelcaan tribe of the West, and our mother is a fierce warrior princess. The Hebelcaan were created by the Gods to be caretakers for horses, or so the legend goes. So now, they roam the countryside, along with their horses, never staying in one place for too long. My father doesn't belong to the tribe, which apparently, grandpa wasn't too happy about. Not like that could stop our mom. Marion tells me that I get my stubbornness from my mother – I just like to think of it as being strong-willed.

We zip through the forest with ease, carefree and lighthearted. After a while, Pax and I do our usual race back to the stables. I beat him by half a stride and take a triumphant bow to my imaginary audience. "Good girl, Nalda," I say giving her a gentle pat. It's difficult leaving Nalda in her stable tonight. I don't want her to think that I've abandoned her and it's not like I can explain to her what's going on. I give her one last carrot for good measure and a pat on her muzzle before heading out.

We take our time walking back to the house, not wanting to let go of this trouble-free feeling. Eventually, we reach the back door and I know that the time has come for me to face reality again.

As we enter the house, the smell of the stew saturates the kitchen and my mouth instantly fills with saliva. The tender mixture of rabbit, potatoes, and mushrooms are a perfect combination, but I can't seem to make myself eat more than a couple of spoonfuls. Marion pretends not to notice and in her best attempt at normality, tries to strike up a conversation about how our first day of school went. Pax chatters away about how excited he is that soccer tryouts are starting, but all I can think about is The Summoning and the chance that I might meet my parents and my other sibling tonight when I travel to the Realm of the Awakened.

"What do you think Dannia is up to these days?" I say, interrupting Pax. He glares at me for a second, but quickly forgives my rudeness.

Complete silence follows. Maybe this isn't considered appropriate dinner conversation?

"Well... I suppose she's still fighting in the war," Marion responds.

"The West needs all of the warriors they can get and by now, she's probably pretty fierce," Kenlin adds. "She's been fighting since she was thirteen, after all."

"I don't remember her. I can't even picture her face," Pax admits.

This breaks my heart. At least I have a vague memory of our older sister. Pax was only two when we were sent here, to the Realm of Somnolence, for protection. It was a desperate decision that our people made to try and ensure our survival. Only some select children and a few guardians were sent here. Dannia was not among those children.

"I still don't understand…how could they send us away?" I ask. "Dangerous or not, I don't see how you can just ship your kids off to another realm." Usually when I start asking questions like these, Marion and Kenlin give me some spiel about how my parents had no choice but to send Pax and me away. That's normally enough to keep me quiet. Tonight is different and I think Kenlin senses it.

"There's more to it than that, Arden," Kenlin responds, pausing to take a deep breath, "I think you're old enough to know. The Bravura are… different."

Marion interrupts, "OK that's *enough*!" She shoots Kenlin a condemning look.

"What do you mean? What are you not telling me?"

"Nothing dear," Marion says, "he just means that the Bravura are different because they were the first of our people to be sent here – the first to be spared from the war."

The look on Kenlin's face tells me that I'm missing something, that Marion isn't telling me the whole truth. I want to ask more, but for some reason I'm afraid to push further. I've never known

Marion to hide anything from me before and I don't really know how to take it.

"Just consider it a blessing that you're part of the Bravura and don't join in the fighting until you're sixteen and deemed ready," Kenlin hastily finishes.

"Of course. I feel *totally* blessed," I reply, laying on the sarcasm as thickly as I can.

I know that I should feel lucky to be a Bravura, but it's more complicated than that. I'm constantly torn between feelings of jealousy and guilt about my life. Jealousy because Dannia got to stay with our parents while I was shipped off to another realm, and guilt about the fact that I've had such an easy life while all this time, she's been fighting for hers.

Marion ends the conversation by abruptly getting up from the table and disappearing into the other room. She returns with a beautiful birthday cake she has baked for me – chocolate with white icing and little yellow roses on top. I do my best to play along and take a few bites of the cake. I don't want her to think that she went through all that trouble of baking such a pretty cake for nothing.

After we finish eating, Marion tells me she has one last surprise, and takes me upstairs to her room. "As your final preparation for tonight you will need to dress the part. It's customary for trainees to don the apparel of their ancestors for The Summoning," she says and pulls out a garment from the wardrobe, an expectant look on her face. Upon closer examination, I see that it's a buckskin dress. The hide looks worn, but it's in good condition. It's not very long and looks as though it laces up the sides. *Is she serious*? I'm not exactly a skirt kind of girl. I take one look at it, walk over to Marion's dresser, pull the shears from her sewing drawer, and proceed to cut the dress in half, transforming it into a much more doable buckskin sleeveless top. The look on Marion's face is priceless. I grab the remains of the dress and confidently stride to my bedroom.

I have a little trouble slipping on the buckskin top and it's definitely itchier than I had expected. I don't think I have anything in my wardrobe that goes with buckskin, so I just pull the first pair of pants I find in my dresser and slip them on. They're nice and comfy – not too tight, just the way I like them. The buckskin top hits just below my belly button and the laces on the sides dangle down a little past my hips. I go over to the full-length mirror I have in my room and do a little twirl, admiring myself. I think this is about the toughest I've ever looked in my life. Even with my twirling. When I return to Marion, I have on a pair of camouflage pants, boots, and the half-cut dress on top. "What? I just thought it could use a little modification," I say.

"I hope you have a better attitude tonight," she says with a sigh.

"I just hope the *Awakened* ones are ready for me," I reply with an air of artificial confidence.

Marion reaches over and cradles my face with both of her hands, "I know you're ready for this my darling. You're stronger than you think." She brushes some loose strands of hair out of my eyes and in that instant I think she still sees me as the little girl she rescued all those years ago. Marion's efforts to soothe me make me realize just how much I'm going to miss her.

After all, she and Kenlin have raised me since I was six years old. I've known no other parents. At least not really. Marion has been the one to comfort me when I had a scraped knee or came down with the flu. Kenlin, never far away, was always quick to chase away the monsters I was certain were hiding under my bed. They have meant as much to me as any blood relative ever could, and now it's time for me to leave them – a thought that I have to admit frightens me. They may think I'm ready for this, but I don't know if I agree.

Night comes quickly. Before I know it we're making our way into the forest. I can feel my heart pounding and the blood coursing through my veins. My chest feels tight and I have to remind myself to breathe. It's even worse knowing that we're going to be close to the spot where we saw the creature this morning. I have to try to block it out of my mind to get myself to keep walking. I hold my talisman for comfort, but I don't think it's helping much. The forest looks different to me in the nighttime – less welcoming, as if it has a secret.

Marion, Kenlin, and Pax are all with me and I can feel the tension radiating off of them. We reach the gnarled oak tree. I see a shallow pit dug into the ground nearby, surrounded by large stones. There are a bunch of logs and sticks arranged in what looks like a mini teepee in the center of the pit. Thoroughly confused, I look over at Kenlin. "I took the liberty of preparing the site earlier today," he explains. I look closer and see that there are markings drawn in the dirt, forming a circle around the pit. I don't recognize most of the markings, but there's one that I've seen before. It's the same design that's on my talisman: a horse emerging from a wave.

Marion takes my hand, "It's time now, dear."

Pax runs over to me and gives me one last hug. He averts his eyes so that they never quite meet mine.

Kenlin grabs me firmly by the shoulders, "Remember, a good tracker can find her way out of a moonless night," he says and steps aside to make room for me to enter the circle. Kenlin lights a torch and hands it to me. I take my place, torch in hand, in the center of the circle near the pit. Marion and Kenlin begin chanting softly, barely above a whisper. At first, I can't make out the words, but the chant becomes increasingly louder. I hear the lines from a story that Marion used to tell me as a child, a story about the Bravura. I start thinking about how strange that seems, but my thoughts are disrupted.

"Now!" Marion shouts and I instinctively toss the torch into the pit. The fire blazes ferociously; orange, yellow, and red flames grip at the night air, struggling for freedom. Suddenly, a single flame shoots out and lands on the image of the horse and the wave that's been sketched into the dirt. The flame spreads rapidly around the other designs surrounding the pit, until I'm encased by a complete circle of fire. The smoke from the fire makes my eyes burn and I start to feel light-headed. The picture before me begins to waver. Everything turns hazy until I can no longer see anything but darkness, and a sharp feeling of fear envelopes me. I feel helpless, consumed by the darkness.

Then, out of the corner of my eye, I see a flicker of light. The flicker dances playfully across my vision, making me dizzy. The haziness returns, but instead of getting darker the picture is getting lighter and clearer. A figure forms in front of me, the outline of what appears to be a man.

A loud booming voice fills my ears, "Welcome Arden Jacinda Khumeia of the Hebelcaan tribe. You have been summoned!"

CHAPTER 3

Hunted

My eyes slowly begin to focus and I notice that something is off. It's light out. I'm no longer standing in darkness, but I now have the bright rays of the sun beating down on me. I realize that dusk at home is dawn in my new realm. *Well this ought to do wonders for my sleep cycle.* I look around and see that I'm standing in a clearing, the remnants of a fire in front of me, and all around the clearing are dense woods.

I can see the man before me clearly now. He has dark skin and black hair and although he is young, no more than a few years older than me, he has a fierce look in his eyes that tells me he's dangerous.

"Do you come here willingly, ready to fight and die for your people?" he asks in a commanding voice.

"Um, yeah," I manage to stammer.

"Will you pledge your life to the Western Kingdoms and continue our fight until your dying breath?"

"Sure?"

The man only then seems to really see me for the first time. A look of disdain spreads across his face. Maybe this was a bad outfit choice after all.

Just then an arrow whizzes by my head, making me jump in surprise.

"Arden Jacinda Khumeia, your training begins!" the man shouts and disappears from sight into the foreboding forest that surrounds us.

Panic. Panic is the only word to describe what I feel. I run in the opposite direction of the origin of the arrow, hoping to find safety in the forest. I'm familiar with forests – how to climb trees, avoid hunting traps, forage and gather. Thanks to Kenlin, my Ranger skills are on point. I'm going to have to try to use that to my advantage since I don't really know what awaits me. *Thanks a lot mysterious stranger – aren't you supposed to be my spirit guide or something?*

As I'm about to reach the edge of the forest, I see a sword sticking up from the ground about a hundred yards off, a red cloth tied around the hilt. This weapon may mean my survival, so I make a beeline for the sword, thinking it must be meant for me. I grab the hilt and yank hard, managing to free the blade from the ground.

A loud, forceful bellow comes from somewhere inside the dense woods, in what I can only interpret as a battle cry. The cry moves closer and before I know it, I'm face-to-face with a sword-wielding maniac in full armor. Well at least I was half-right. The sword is definitely meant for me. Whether or not it helps me survive is another story.

Not wasting any time, my assailant swings at me with brute force. I'm taken aback by his desire to kill me, as if my mere existence offends him. I'm able to dodge the blow by rolling behind a tree and he misses the top of my head by a fraction. His sword sticks in the trunk of the unsuspecting tree and while he furiously attempts to dislodge his weapon, I take a swing at him. The weight of the sword feels good in my hands and I hit him hard on his breastplate; not enough to do any real damage, but enough that I knock the wind out of him. I quickly decide that it's in my best interest to make my escape while I can, so I run deeper into the forest, taking erratic turns to lose my pursuer. I continue running as fast as my legs will carry me for what seems like an eternity. When I feel I have enough distance between us, I slow my run to catch my breath and take inventory of my surroundings.

I notice that the trees are different from the ones we have back at home. For one thing, they're huge. From their height, it looks like they've been growing for thousands of years. Also, their leaves are a beautiful bluish green color like nothing I've ever seen before on a tree – like little turquoise gemstones. The canopy above my head looks like an ocean, the waves forming as the leaves move along with the breeze. It's mesmerizing.

As I keep walking, I find myself wishing that I'd worn a newer pair of boots on this fantastic voyage. My favorite boots, the ones I'm currently wearing, are so worn-out that I can already feel the blisters forming on the soles of my feet. I try to ignore the pain and keep walking deeper into the woods.

The sound of a nearby stream exacerbates the burning in my throat. I need water. My muscles start shaking a little from dehydration as I continue to walk. It's clear I haven't trained nearly enough. Anger floods my brain. Anger at my own arrogance and lack of preparation.

I hastily make my way towards the sound until I reach the stream. I let the sword in my hand fall to the ground. My less-than-obliging body betrays me as I bend down to take a sip, causing me to splash face first into the cool water. I reach my shaky hand into the stream, cupping the liquid and bringing it towards my pleading lips. I instantly feel refreshed the moment the water flows down my aching throat.

Before I have the chance to take another drink, my ponytail is nearly cut in half by the tip of an arrow as it breezes past my head.

I jump behind a nearby boulder, sword in hand. My body shakes violently with a mixture of adrenalin and fear. I try to control my limbs, but I can't. WHOOSH! Another arrow whizzes by my face. I stay low and scramble to the other side of the rock, hoping that it will shield me from my assailant. I wish Kenlin were here. He would know what to do. What do I know about archery attacks? I know that arrows move in a straight line, which means that if I can anticipate where they are coming from, I can protect myself. I also know that I have to keep moving. PING! An arrow bounces off the side of the boulder right next to where I'm crouched. The archer must be on the move! I ignore my body's desire to curl up into a ball and force myself up. I must find safety. I start running for my life, trying to keep the trees between me and where I think the archer is located. I only make it several yards away when another arrow hits. The arrows are coming every few seconds. I start running again, but this time I keep count while I run. One…two…three…THUD! An arrow strikes a tree. I have four seconds. It takes the archer exactly four seconds to pull another arrow from his quiver, nock, and fire his weapon. I must plan my moves accordingly. One…two…I search for the closest tree…THUD! It strikes the tree about a foot above my head. Little turquoise gems fall around my feet. Now's my time to move. I see my next target – a tree located diagonally to my right. One…I may have underestimated the distance of the tree…two…I throw the sword ahead of me and dive to the ground, rolling behind the base of the tree. WHOOSH! The arrow flies above me while I roll.

I close my eyes and listen to the forest. The forest will tell me what I need to know. I hear no footsteps. I hear no voices. The archer must be far away or I would hear him moving as he changes the direction of his arrows. Unless there is more than one archer. Based on the timing of the arrows and only minor directional adjustments, I believe there to be only one, but I can't be sure.

What count am I on?

THUD! The archer lets me know my time is up. I grab my sword off the ground and sprint as fast as I can. Without looking, I take a flying leap into what appears to be a large ditch, just barely managing to avoid an arrow to the neck.

I immediately regret my decision. The ditch is pretty deep, its edges just exceeding my 5'7" frame, and it's shaped like a rectangle.

Although it's too wide for a grave, it's hauntingly similar. The arrows have ceased.

It's too late before I realize that whoever is shooting the arrows has been deliberately directing me to this spot. The tiny clicking of their legs as they scuttle towards me is my first warning of their presence. To my horror, I see hundreds of giant black beetles coming towards me. Their bodies are larger than normal and they have sharp, ferocious pincers. I try to scramble back up the side of the ditch, but I'm not quite strong enough to pull myself up on the first try. I slip back down the side, my fingers leaving a trail in the dirt. The horrible creatures begin to crawl up my leg. I try to bat them away with my sword, but they're too quick and the first of the bites make me wail out in pain. Trying to outmaneuver them, I claw my way back up the side of the dirt wall and heave myself out. By the time I escape, I have about fifteen bites on my legs and arms. My limbs are red and throbbing, but I'm relieved to see that the beetles are not able to leave the ditch, and for the moment, the arrows are leaving me alone. I compel myself to stand and walk even though the pain of the bites makes me wince with each step.

I take deep, slow breaths. In the nose, out of the mouth. I try to steady my hands. Will they ever stop shaking?

What kind of sick training method is this anyway? I'm no good to the West if I die in training. It still feels like the bugs are crawling all over my skin even though I know they're back in the grave-like ditch where they belong.

Exhaustion begins to set in. I haven't slept since last night and it must be getting late back home. Pax is probably snuggled up with Sasha right now. I wish I was in my own bed instead of out here in these harsh woods covered in beetle bites and struggling to walk. I waited sixteen years for this? Maybe it was naïve to expect them to be waiting for me, but it was the one thing that made the idea of coming to this realm bearable. Where are they? Then a thought occurs to me. Maybe my parents and my sister didn't want to come see me.

Insecurity begins to creep up inside me, infecting my brain and trying to suck away what little strength I have left. I have to fight it with all of my power. I must keep my head in the game or I won't make it out of here. I have to remind myself that I was chosen for a reason, that I'm one of the Bravura.

Before I start feeling too sorry for myself, out of nowhere another arrow whirs by and interrupts my thoughts. The fear comes rushing back in an all-consuming wave. I run. One…two…three…WHOOSH. I duck behind a tree. I don't want to be led into another trap. Do I dare try and go against the arrows' command? I decide to try something crazy and start running in the direction of the arrow's origin, trying to stay behind the trees as I run. One…two…three…THUMP! An arrow lands just in front of my feet. The archer is warning me. Find a new direction. I run to a tree and press my back up against the trunk. In the nose, out of the mouth. I run. Two…three…my back is pressed against the next tree. THUD! I listen. I must locate the archer. Where is he? I hear a whinny off in the distance. A horse! My opponent is on a horse! I remember a call Kenlin taught me to do whenever I want Gala or Nalda to come. I click my tongue, stick a finger on each side of my mouth and blow. A loud whistle fills the woods. I hear the horse neigh loudly in response. I poke my head out from behind the tree and look ahead, planning out my next moves. Click, whistle. The horse is agitated. It wants to come to me. I know this because I can hear a rustle in the forest as if the rider can't control his steed. He is distracted now. I run toward the sound, keeping count in my head, ducking behind trees all the while. It takes me a minute or so before I notice that the arrows are no longer coming at me and the sound of the horse has disappeared. I stop behind a tree. I wait a full one hundred and fifty seconds before walking out into the open.

I take advantage of the respite and slow my pace to a walk to conserve my energy. I make a mental note to find the source of those arrows if given another chance.

While I'm walking, I see a bronze shield lying against a tree. Another red cloth is tied to the enarmes of the shield, just like it had been on the sword. This time I hesitate before picking it up. Did the swordsman jump out at me because I picked up the sword or was the sword there so that I could protect myself? My question is quickly answered when before I even touch the shield, an oversized woman comes barreling at me from behind a tree, swinging a ball and chain wildly about. The weapon, or flail as Kenlin taught me, is a metal rod with a ball and chain attached. There are malicious spikes protruding from the ball. This weapon is definitely *not* a toy and I can only assume that she means to cause some serious damage. The woman looks strong, but I have to think that I'm quicker. I run to the tree and snatch up the shield, preparing to defend myself. Paired with my sword, I pray that I may actually have a chance of making it through this alive.

"I hope you're ready to die little one," she says in a mocking tone. "You Bravura have been dropping like flies lately and by the looks of you, you're not going to last long here!"

"Why don't you pick on someone your own…"

BOOM! The flail smashes into my shield, making a circular dent. She takes another eager swing and I'm able to block it once again, although the force from her strike brings me to my knees. My body shakes. I try to make myself believe it's from the strain of the hit.

One of the spikes punctures the shield, landing about an inch from my face. She pulls back her flail, taking my shield with it.

The woman lets out a cruel laugh, "Is that all you have, little Bravura?" she says and tosses my shield carelessly aside while preparing to take another swing.

I feel something inside my head snap. The rage swells up inside my chest. I've had about enough of this, and I'm tired of playing by their rules. While she winds up the flail for another blow, I jump to my feet, ready to face her. My hands are steady.

She catches nothing but air this time as I roll under her wild swing. Before she can prepare for another one, I lunge forward from my crouched position, stabbing my sword into her leg. Direct strike. *Oh my god.* I've never actually used a weapon against somebody in such a real way before and I'm surprised at how easily the blade slices through her skin like it's nothing more than warm butter. I feel like gagging when I see the blood start trickling out of the spot where the blade entered her leg. I stand there, stunned.

She cries out in pain, bringing me back to reality. The wound is enough to make her drop the flail to her side. While her attention is on her leg, I take a swing at the flail with my sword, knocking it away from her. I want this fight to be over. I'm not quite used to these weapons though and I lose my balance for just a second, leaning the tip of the sword into the ground to catch myself from falling. Our eyes meet and I see nothing but anger looking back at me.

Before I can regain my balance, the woman takes her large fist and punches me square in the face with the kind of punch that would make a heavy-weight champion proud.

The world around me goes black.

CHAPTER 4

Nursery Rhymes

I wake up lying on a cot in what appears to be a makeshift hospital, with no memory of how I got here. The constant throbbing of my eye brings back flashes of my unsuccessful boxing debut – too bad my training at home didn't include getting punched in the face, maybe I would've lasted a few more rounds.

I'm in a small white room comprised of thin canvas walls. I think that the walls are put up more as a courtesy for the tenants than for any real function – they do little to keep out the noise and I can see outlines of people darting around. A young woman wearing a white linen gown is standing over me, applying a cool cream to my bites. "There now, does that feel better?" she says, looking down at me with a soft expression. "I'm afraid there isn't much more I can do for that eye. The swelling has gone down quite a bit, but the bruising may be there for another day or two. You really should be more careful."

"Uh, thanks," I say, as I try to get up, perturbed at the implication that my wounded eye is somehow my fault.

"Just wait here for a moment. Marcus will be here soon enough to escort you back," she says, ignoring my scowl.

The woman leaves me alone in the hospital and the quiet is too much for my tired body. I quickly slip away into unconsciousness.

I'm not sure how long I've been asleep before the sounds of explosions fill my ears. The smoke from the blasts is thick, blanketing the world around me and making it hard to see and even harder to breathe. I'm running now as fast as my legs will take me towards a hill I can just make out in the distance. The searing heat from the explosions burns my back as I run. Someone is chasing me, but the smoke makes it impossible to see who. I'm frightened. As I approach the base of the hill, a ball of fire flies towards my head and I scream. The distraction causes me to miss the giant tree root sticking out of the ground in front of me, and I trip and fall, tumbling forward. I'm desperately clutching my bag with all of my strength, trying my best not to let go of it, when the clanging of armor being thrown on the ground startles me awake.

I bolt upright in my cot with a gasp and see that the man who first greeted me in the clearing is standing before me.

"I didn't mean to startle you," he says, amused.

"No, I wasn't startled... I was, uh, just resting my eyes for a minute." Can't a girl catch a break? I can't believe that this incessant nightmare has followed me here. Running for my life isn't my idea of a good time. And why am I trying so hard to hold onto that bag? I mean, it isn't even cute. I'm sure there are more interesting things to dream about.

"It's OK, you need the rest. You'll be brought here each day at the end of training so that the healers can tend to your wounds and you can rest before returning to your realm," the man explains. "By the way, my name is Marcus."

"It's nice to meet you, Marcus. I'm sorry we weren't properly introduced earlier, you know, when I was running for my life."

"Yes, well we have a learn-as-you-go method of training here. We feel our trainees learn faster that way. Plus, it tends to weed out the weak ones early," he says as he looks me over. "We're trying to be more careful with who we send out to battle these days. Cut down on the number of casualties."

While I usually appreciate directness, I think I could use some sugar coating right about now.

He continues, "You really tore into Tarla's leg today. I'm not sure she's going to forgive you anytime soon."

Is that a look of admiration I see flash across his face? "I'm going to assume Tarla is the one who gave me this lovely new addition," I say pointing to my black eye. "Is she OK?" As much as I'm peeved that she was trying to bash my head in with a spikey ball, I still feel really bad about the whole leg thing.

"Who? Tarla? It takes more than a stab wound in the leg to slow her down, although, if you do see her again, I recommend going in the opposite direction."

Great, I'm already making friends. Guess I can't blame her for being mad. "Does this mean that I'm finished with my training and I can go home now?"

"Yes, you're finished for today; however, we have a few more items to go over before you return." Marcus reaches behind him and pulls something from a bag. When he turns to face me, he has a large book and a small golden object in his hands. He hands me the book. "Here, this is your guide book. It contains everything you need to know about the Western Kingdom's territories, the types of creatures that exist in this realm, and the kinds of Eastern adversaries you may face. Study this book. It may mean the difference between life and death for you."

"Thanks," I say reaching for the book, not thrilled about the extra homework. "What else do you have there?"

He tosses the golden object playfully in the air and I see that it's a gold coin. "This here is your ticket back home. You will use it to travel back and forth between realms."

"What? No bonfire party this time?" I ask, attempting to lighten the mood.

"The fire is only required for The Summoning. The ceremony allows us to direct you to a specific location. Now that you've travelled to this realm, you'll be able to come back to the very same spot where you first arrived. All you have to do is picture it in your mind and say the spell."

"Spell? I don't know any spells."

"Actually, you do," he corrects. "You see, this coin has been enchanted so that The Call of the Bravura will trigger your transport."

"And what, may I ask, is The Call of the Bravura?" Clearly, Marcus and I are not on the same page.

"It goes a little something like this, "Take me home, take me home…""

"Wait!" I interrupt, recognizing the words that Marion and Kenlin were chanting at the fire during The Summoning. "Isn't that from a children's storybook?"

"Yes…very good! You just may make it through training after all," he says and chuckles to himself. "There's much more to that fable than meets the eye. Do you remember The Call?"

I search my memory, trying to remember the sing-songy words that Marion used to recite to me and Pax. In an instant, they come rushing back:

To a land far away with secrets unknown,

The children were sent with no family or home.

With hopes for them to grow big and strong,

Knowing no fear; away from all harm.

The Bravura they will be named, for brave they shall be,

On their shoulders will rest the fate of you and me.

One day ready to join in the fight,

The children will say with all of their might:

"Take me home; take me home, I'm calling to you now, for I'm in a land where I do not belong. I feel the plea of my people deep in my bones and the only answer is to take me back home."

"Yes, I remember it. All I have to do is hold the coin and repeat the words and it'll take me back home?"

"That's about it. Just remember to picture the spot where you want to go to. This type of transport is used by all of the Bravura to allow travel between realms. Oh, one more thing," he says before reaching behind him again, "take this to carry your things in. It too is enchanted and will protect whatever it holds."

I reach out to accept his offering and my heart leaps into my throat. It's unmistakable. In his hands is the very same bag that has been haunting me every night in my dreams.

CHAPTER 5

Training Camp

Reluctantly, I take the bag from Marcus and stand up ready to leave the hospital and go home. The burning sensation in my legs and arms has disappeared and I feel surprisingly well-rested. Marcus walks me through the hospital, which is really just a giant white tent divided into several smaller rooms. The doorway to each room is blocked by a curtain. The hallway itself is filled with people dressed in white linen who are rushing in and out of the many rooms. Their uniforms are covered with fresh blood and they have pained looks on their faces. The contrast of the bright red stains on the snow-colored linen sends shivers down my spine. I don't want to know where the blood came from.

To my left and right, additional hallways stretch far down the line. There must be hundreds of people hidden away in these rooms. The constant wailing cutting through the air and the stench of infection permeating the flimsy canvas make me think some of the people here are seriously injured. Maybe even dying. I guess I should feel lucky I'm not one of them.

A commotion is coming from one of the nearby rooms. There appears to be a heated discussion taking place. As we get closer I hear a woman's voice. It's raspy and weak, as if she's been shouting. "Another one has gone missing just this morning. Didn't even make it to her first battle. We don't know how it happened – there were two third plane wizards with her."

A gruff male voice replies, "That's the second one this week. Can't be good."

"She'd only just completed her training. Her sister went missing about a month ago, too. We think the East must have known where we were taking her. I've told Marcus to call a meeting with the Elders."

When we walk by, I peek inside and see two burly men and a slim young woman dressed in battle gear. She looks worried and fatigued, worn-out. I try to stop for a second, but Marcus hurries me along the corridor and out of the hospital.

Fields of bright green grass are waiting for us outside of the tent. The training camp itself is much larger than I thought when I first arrived. They must have had me tucked away in my own special section just for newbies.

By the looks of the hardened people walking through this place, I probably wouldn't stand a chance against any of them in a fight. Most are around my age, although some older folks are tossed in the mix too. There's an assortment of costumes floating around, including tough-looking armor, buckskin uniforms like the one Marion tried to get me to wear, and some plain linen clothes as well. I wonder how long some of these other kids have been in training and if they're tired of it yet. Having people try to kill you every day must start to wear on you at some point.

Marcus guides me through the bustling crowd for what seems like miles. We weave our way through the various tents. Some are used for housing, with small cots lined up in neat little rows like military barracks. Another looks to hold today's kill, probably for dinner later. The obscene amount of animal carcasses hanging from the ceiling compels me to look away. It's confirmed – there will be no tofu for me in this realm.

A few feet ahead of us there's a school where a group of kids are furiously writing with feather quills as an older man dressed in long robes lectures. I think the topic must relate to botany since he's pointing to a table displaying several unfamiliar plants. The man touches a fiery red, star-shaped flower with his pointer and it spits a yellow liquid from its center, making the class jump in their seats. The liquid sizzles on the ground, giving off yellow-tinted fumes. The scent of lemons fills the air and a kid near the front of the room faints. The teacher hurries over and pulls him away from the fumes, fanning the kid's blank face.

Marcus pulls me along and as we continue to walk, I notice one aspect of the camp that's especially disturbing. Interspersed in the crowd, every so often, an unlucky soul who's been disfigured in some way will fly past us on a stretcher, his or her injury revealing the brutal cost of war. There are too many to count. The ones that cry out in pain are disturbing, those that don't are even more so.

I'm shaken by what I've seen, but I don't want Marcus to think I'm weak, so I hold it in. I have a feeling the weak ones don't make it out of this place in one piece. I'm good at holding things in.

Metal weapons glisten in a large tent on my left. They stand leaning against one another in an organized mess, looking harmless. They are not. An absurdly muscular man, sweaty and covered in black filth, stands out in front of the artillery tent next to a fire. His massive frame casts a large, domineering shadow; his leather apron looks miniscule. He doesn't even see us as he hammers away at the yellow and orange glowing tip of a sword resting atop an anvil. Sparks fly with each powerful strike of the hammer, but the man doesn't flinch. He cannot be distracted, he is death's designer and he's busy creating.

We reach the clearing in the woods where I first entered this mysterious world. The quietness of the clearing is a stark contrast to the bustle of the tent-filled training site. Daytime is drawing to a close, the light saying its last farewells as the sun sets in the distance. Vibrant hues of orange, pink, and red fill the sky. The orange and pink are lovely, calming. I have had enough of red.

"Till tomorrow, Arden Jacinda Khumeia," Marcus says, clasping my shoulder with his strong hand.

Gathering that this is where I'm supposed to take my leave, I grab the coin from my bag and begin to think about the old gnarled oak tree back in the forest where this all started. It's not hard to imagine since I desperately want to go back there. Closing my eyes, I hesitate a moment before reciting the familiar words from my childhood, "Take me home; take me home, I'm calling to you now, for I'm in a land where I do not belong. I feel the plea of my people deep in my bones and the only answer is to take me back home." As I finish speaking the last word, I feel a pull in my gut as if I'm being tugged, willed forward by some invisible force. All of the breath is forced out of me and I begin coughing and gasping for air. When I manage to regain control, I see that I'm back in my forest right next to the ugly old gnarled oak tree. I've never been so happy to see a tree before. I jump up in excitement and hug the old thing. Realizing that I've taken the term "tree-hugger" to a new level, I let out a little laugh and head for home.

CHAPTER 6

Electricity

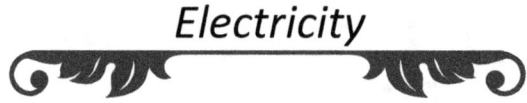

When I reach the house, I try to enter as quietly as possible. Judging from the light, I figure it must be early morning. I gently open the door and take a few cautious steps before I hear, "Oh thank goodness! You made it back!"

"Ahhh!" I reply to the greeting as my body tenses from surprise. "Marion! You scared me! What are you doing awake already?"

Marion runs over and wraps her arms tightly around me, "Like I could sleep on your first day. You must tell me everything! But first, hurry upstairs and wash up. You don't want to be late for school."

"School? Seriously? Don't I even get a free pass *today*?"

"The quicker you learn that there are no free passes in life, the better." With a concerned look, she reaches out her hand and lightly touches the edge of my eye. "I see that you made quite an impression on your first day."

"Oh, right, I almost forgot. I uh, made a new friend," I say with a forced smile and head upstairs to clean up.

On the way to my room, I stop by Pax's door and see that he's sound asleep. I walk over to his bed and gingerly kiss him on the top of his head. He would kill me if he knew, but I'm so grateful to see him again that I don't care.

I feel the grime of the night's adventures cloaking my body and I want nothing more than to wash away the evidence of my double life. I tip-toe my way to the shower and turn on the water, making the temperature as hot as my skin can take. The steam from the water surrounds me and I shut my eyes. I take this moment for myself. I have to remind myself that I'm still me. I'm still Arden. Even if I have this other side to me, this Bravura side, I'm still just a sixteen-year-old girl. And right now I have to go to school.

After showering, I put on my school uniform and walk outside to meet Derek. For some reason, I can't stop thinking about the conversation I overheard at the training camp. Are Bravura disappearing? Do I need to add this to my list of imminent dangers in this new life?

When I get outside, I see that Kenlin is already sitting by the garage, occupied with making a new bow. His skilled hands are working his knife along the natural curve of the wood, slowly forming the shape of the bow. He cranes his neck to look up at me. "I see you didn't waste any time getting in on the action," he says with a grin. "You're starting to look like a real warrior. Keep up the good work."

"Yeah, I'll have to tell you all about it sometime. Training was a real treat."

Derek is walking out to his car when he sees me coming towards him. His face falls instantly and he drops his books to the ground. Rushing over to me, flushed, his words come pouring out of his mouth. "What happened to you? Are you OK? Did someone hit you?" He grabs me by the shoulders, "I swear, whoever did this to you…"

"It's OK. I'm OK," I insist. Trying to think up a quick explanation, I find myself saying, "I just fell off my horse last night when Pax and I were racing through the woods." The excuse sounds lame as it's coming out of my mouth, especially considering that Derek knows I'm an expert rider, but I've never been very good at lying. And I've never lied to Derek before. I guess there's a first for everything.

He seems to buy it, which only adds to my guilt. "Oh," he sighs in relief. "You know you should really be more careful when you take your horse out at night. There's no reason for you to do any more damage to that face of yours – it's already damaged enough as it is," he says, holding his hands up in mock defense, anticipating my reaction.

"Ha, ha very funny," I reply.

He takes his hand and brushes the back of it gently against the bruised area on my face. "What *am* I going to do with you, AJ?" he asks softly.

"Let's start with taking me to school," I reply, trying my best to sound chipper.

We arrive at school and it hits me that I have to walk around with a busted face all day. Great.

When I walk up to the front of the school building I feel like I'm in one of those movie scenes where everybody stops and looks when the pretty girl walks in – except this time, everybody's stopping to gawk at my swollen eye. Not exactly the kind of attention I need.

A group of nearby girls turns to look at me and they start giggling to each other. Cici is among them, but instead of giggling she's eyeing me up and down like I just tried to steal her boyfriend. I brush it off and accept that this is going to be a rough day.

I'm running a little late for first period, but I decide to take a detour to the girls' bathroom anyway. I want to see if adding concealer to my eye will help mask this horrible purple color. It takes me several attempts before I'm forced to concede that this is the best I'm going to look for the day.

I know that my efforts have been futile when I enter the classroom because I hear several gasps and the chatter noticeably picks up before I claim my seat near the back of the room. I figure that my eye must be an exciting topic of conversation compared to the usual boring gossip.

"You're late," an unfamiliar voice purrs from the seat next to me.

My natural defensive side kicks in and I turn, ready with a retort, but my voice catches in my throat when I see who's there. It's him –

Zeke – with his intense green eyes, looking directly at me. I feel the blood rush to my face, my cheeks reddening, and I'm suddenly very conscious of what this new onset of blood will do to my already black and blue eye.

"Why do you care? You're not even supposed to be in this class," I finally manage to spit out.

He raises the corner of one eyebrow, surprised at my instant hostility. "Just looking out for you is all. I transferred from Creative Writing," he says. Pausing and leaning in towards me as if what he's about to say is strictly confidential, "I thought this class would be more *interesting*," he whispers.

I feel a shiver of electricity shoot up my spine when he gets close to me, jolting me to my senses. His deep, soft voice is so... alluring. I want him to say more. To keep the conversation going, I just blurt out the first thing that comes to mind, "I don't know why anyone would volunteer to take History with Mr. Gerber. He's known for being super harsh."

"Thanks for the insight. I think I could learn a lot from you," he replies with no hint of playfulness in his tone.

"Enough back there!" shouts Mr. Gerber, drawing our attention away from each other and forcing us to turn and face the front of the room.

For the remainder of the class I find myself stealing glances of Zeke out of the corner of my eye. I try to control it, but I can't. It's like there's an energy drawing me closer to him. I catch him doing the same. It seems that both of us are mutually curious about one another.

The bell rings, ending my torture. I don't think that I heard one thing the teacher said all class. History is definitely going to be a problem for me with this type of distraction around.

I get up from my desk and on my way out of the classroom Zeke grabs my wrist and pulls me close to him. His grip is strong and forceful. He bends down so that his lips are dangerously close to my left ear – I can practically feel them brushing my earlobe as he speaks. "You really should take better care of yourself, Arden," he hisses angrily and motions towards my eye. His breath feels hot on my neck, and the vibration of his voice against my skin gives me goose bumps. The touch of his hand makes all the tiny hairs on my arm stand up as if electrified. I'm surprised at how incredibly alive I feel standing this near to him.

"Yeah, uh, I know. I fell off my horse. Sorry?" I say in a questioning tone, since I don't know what he wants me to tell him. Why I feel the need to apologize to him at all, I'm not quite sure. It's my eye after all.

"Sure, whatever. Just be more careful," he says sternly, almost like he's my parent, and rushes out of the classroom.

I still feel the aftereffects of Zeke's touch as I stand momentarily dazed. I look down at my arm, at the spot where he had grasped it, trying to make sense of it all. His touch felt so different.

Emily is standing outside the classroom door and I can tell she saw the whole thing. I've known her since the third grade, so I can pretty much guess what she's about to say and I'm already embarrassed even before she speaks. "*What* was that all about, Ms. Arden?" she asks excitedly, her strawberry-blond curls bouncing up and down, in sync with her tiny frame.

"That? That was nothing," I say, a little too quickly. Then I think about it for a second. "Actually, I'm not sure what that was."

"Well, I can't believe that gorgeous guy is in your class! You are *so* lucky. Everybody's talking about him, you know."

Derek sneaks up behind me and grabs me by the shoulders, startling me. "What are you two so excited about?"

Emily claps her hands together and giggles, "Just that the hottest guy in school seems to have shown some interest in our little Arden."

"What are you talking about?" Derek asks, noticeably agitated.

"Oh, nothing," I say. "Emily's just exaggerating." Why make a big deal over nothing, right?

"No, I am not! You wait, I'd bet money that he asks you out before the month is over!" she says to me.

"Well, that doesn't mean anything. I mean, it's not like Arden would fall for a guy like that anyway," Derek replies.

Arden. He used my full name, which he never does unless he's mad at me.

"Oh, please. Who *wouldn't* fall for that guy? Just give it some time!" Emily trills and waves goodbye as she makes her way to her next class.

"Seriously, she's being ridiculous. Just forget it. How was English class?" I say hoping to change the subject and improve Derek's mood.

Derek turns to me, concern written all over his face. "You wouldn't... never mind." I'm about to say something when he turns his back to me and heads off to class, leaving me standing in the hallway alone.

To my relief, the afternoon is less eventful and goes by without a hitch – minus the part where I fall asleep in Calculus class. I'm definitely *not* getting off to a good start with Mr. Stein.

I'm beginning to realize that keeping up with classes between Bravura training is going to be much harder than I anticipated. I can barely pay attention in school when I'm at 100%, let alone after a long night of running for my life.

At the end of the day, I'm still thinking about first period – my conversation with Zeke was pretty weird, but Derek's reaction was even stranger. I guess I can see how Derek might be upset – I don't like it when girls flirt with him – but I don't understand why he was *that* upset. Maybe he just doesn't like Zeke? I'm going over everything in my head for the hundredth time when I practically walk straight into Cici.

"Whoa there! Earth to Arden!" Her high-pitched voice is soft and pleasant.

"Hey, sorry. I didn't see you there. Wait, how do you know who I am?"

"This school isn't *that* big, honey. Besides, my brother mentioned he has a class with you," she responds sharply.

Zeke was actually talking about me? This news makes me absurdly excited. I really have to get a grip.

"Right, well sorry for running into you," I reply, trying to sound as nonchalant as possible.

"Oh, no worries. I was hoping that we'd have a chance to chat."

Just then Zeke walks up to us, his movements graceful and controlled. He places his hand gently on the small of my back, which makes my body instantly come alive. "Hey sis," he addresses Cici, "are you over here bothering Arden? I'm sure she has better things to do than stand around talking to you."

"Why hello, *brother*, Arden and I were just getting acquainted," she replies.

Emily walks by with a huge grin on her face and gives me a discreet two thumbs up as she passes us. It seems that when it comes to Zeke, she's not going to be much help bringing me back down to reality.

With his hand still in its place on my back, Zeke looks at me and says in all seriousness, "You can tell me the truth, Arden. Is Cici holding you up?"

There's something about the way my name sounds coming out of his mouth that makes my knees go weak. It takes me a second or two to regain full control over my verbal capabilities.

"No, but I do see my ride coming this way, so I should get going," I manage to say as I spot Derek leaving the school building.

Derek looks up in time to see me standing next to Zeke and Cici. He quickly puts his head down and walks straight to his car, not even acknowledging me as he walks by.

CHAPTER 7

Teamwork

The ride home from school is torturous. Derek refuses to tell me what's wrong and each time I ask he replies with some variation of "Nothing. I'm fine." I try making small talk, but am similarly unsuccessful. Derek and I have been mad at each other before, but it only lasts an hour or so and then we make up as it if had never happened. With everything going on right now, I don't think I can take Derek being mad at me for much longer. I'm counting the minutes until that magical moment when his anger dissipates and we're back to normal.

After what feels like hours, we arrive back at home. Derek shuts off the car's ignition, says, "See ya," and practically hurls himself out. I manage a meek "See ya" in return before the car door shuts in my face. Part of me wants to run after him, but I know Derek well enough to give him some space.

I'm still not sure what I did, but I need to go clear my head before training. I slowly head out to the stables, dragging my feet a bit, and the sight of the old red barn that houses Nalda and Gala

immediately bestows a feeling of calm over me. I often sneak away to the loft on the second floor and just lie there, looking down at our horses as they rest. I like the quiet and privacy it provides, but I doubt I'll have time for that today.

The hay crunches beneath my feet as I walk inside the barn and Nalda greets me with a happy half-snort, half-whinny. Pax is already inside brushing Gala when I arrive and when he sees me he runs up and hugs me so hard that he lifts me about a foot off the ground. *Jeez, he's getting strong.*

"You're back!" he says, the enthusiasm in his voice filling the barn. "What happened? Did you see mom and dad? Was Dannia there?"

"No, I didn't see them. It was strange. It was like as soon as I arrived everyone wanted to kill me."

"Makes sense," he jokingly responds. "What happened to your eye? Is that part of toughening you up for battle or something?"

"Yeah something like that."

"Gotchya. Well you don't look so bad. Could be worse," he says. "Do you have time for a ride? I've got Gala and Nalda all ready to go."

"Good question, Paxy. Come to think of it, I have no idea how much time I have. I can hang out here for a few minutes, but I'm not sure if there's enough time for a ride. This whole thing doesn't exactly come with a manual, you know?" And then it hits me. It *does* come with a manual. A manual that they gave me last night, which I haven't even opened, let alone taken the time to read.

Pax lowers his eyes and purses his lips together. "That's OK. We'll go later some time."

"I think that's a good idea. I might be late already and I wanna wait until at least my second day before screwing up. Take Nalda out for a ride for me will you?" I say, already halfway out the barn door.

"Sure. Catch ya later."

I bound towards the house at an ungodly pace, not even stopping when Sasha tries desperately to distract me with the worn out tennis ball she drops at my feet. I search my room for the bag Marcus gave me. I know it's in here somewhere. *Why does Marion always have to pick up after me?*

Then, I spot it hanging innocently on the back of my desk chair. I wrench the book out of the bag and flip it open – *what no Table of Contents? Who wrote this stupid thing?* I start skimming through the book as fast as I can. What I'm looking for is right there in the first chapter – "Each day at sunset the Bravura will call to their home and the aether will answer, bringing them to their destination." I have no idea what aether is, but I think it's pretty clear that I have until the sun sets to leave for camp – which means that I have about thirty minutes to make it to the tree. I am not going to be late. Thank god. I think I should head out there a little early in case I have trouble getting my coin to work or something. I don't want to take any chances. I hastily put my half-dress and camo pant combination back on – freshly washed thanks to Marion – and grab my bag. Flying down the stairs, I breeze past Marion, who's in the kitchen making dinner.

"Wait!" she yells. "Sit down. You have to eat something."

"But…"

"No buts. You have to make time to eat a little dinner. You need to keep up your strength." She places a plate of pasta and grilled vegetables before me. "Now eat."

"Thanks, Marion," I say and begin to wolf the food down. I am much hungrier than I thought I was and eat so quickly that I can barely taste the pasta. I eat just enough so that I'm full but not overly stuffed. I need to be light on my feet to make it through training and a belly full of pasta isn't going to help. "Thanks for dinner. See ya in the morning!" I say to Marion when I'm done. I start my sprint to the forest as I race against the setting sun. I reach the oak tree just as the sun is beginning to disappear in the horizon, pull out the gold coin and repeat The Call of the Bravura. The tugging of my insides begins – not quite painful, but not comfortable. The next thing I know, the breath in my lungs is sucked out by some invisible force, making me gasp. In a blink, I'm back in the clearing. This is really going to take some time to get used to.

I'm crumpled on the ground coughing when Marcus approaches me. "You're late."

"Yeah, I've been hearing that a lot today," I reply between coughs.

"Don't let it happen again. Now, stand up and face me." I figure Marcus is not the type to ask twice, so I pull myself up off the ground. "Today you'll focus on battle tactics. The objective is for

you and your team to make it to the other side of the forest before nightfall."

That's it? My whole goal is to make it to the other side alive? This can't be good.

Wait a minute. "You said me and my *team*?"

"Yes, we must all learn to work together if we're to defeat the Eastern armies. This is a crucial part of your training. Let me introduce you to some of your fellow Bravura."

Marcus steps aside and I see a boy and a girl. Both look to be my age and both are absurdly dressed in what I'm beginning to recognize as the standard attire for this realm. They're standing near one another, but slightly awkwardly, as if they don't know what to do with themselves.

"These two have been training a bit longer than you, but they, like you, have a long way to go. You'll have five minutes to deliberate and plan your strategy," Marcus says before disappearing again into the forest.

That guy is starting to seem like a one-man vanishing act. I may have to start calling him Marcus the Mysterious.

The boy, who's dressed in a basic off-white wool tunic, is nervously shifting his weight from one leather sandal clad foot to the other. While the girl, who's wearing a short leather skirt, vest, and boots, is eyeing up my outfit, clearly jealous of my ingenuity. Neither one of them seems happy to be wearing a dress.

"Hey, it's nice to meet you. I'm Arden," I say, hoping to break the ice with my phenomenal conversational skills.

"I'm Kayla," The girl replies. She's tall and muscular, with mocha colored skin and jet-black curly hair. Even though she's wearing a skirt, I'm pretty sure she could kick my butt without even breaking a sweat.

The boy, pale and covered in freckles, with bright red wild-looking hair, walks over and extends his hand. "My name is Trion, pleasure to meet you, Arden. So, what guild are you from?"

"Guild?"

"Yeah, you know, like Kayla here is a huntress. Her family stems from the Animal Masters' Guild, while my family's part of the Wizards' Guild. So... what's your forte?"

"I'm not really sure."

"She must be too new," Kayla chimes in. "Don't worry, you'll figure it out as you go through training. Your skills will kind of just start showing up. Nothing to it."

"Nice! So I'm like a super hero with special powers?" I ask out of sheer excitement at the possibility. *I knew it!*

"No, no it's not like that," Trion says with a chuckle. "It's more like you'll find out that you just have a knack for doing something. Like Kayla here can control animals after only a short while of training and I'm learning how to channel aether."

"Aether. I saw that word in the book they gave me. What's it mean?"

"We really don't have time for this," Kayla interrupts. "Marcus said we only have five minutes to come up with a plan."

Trion responds, "That's true, we should focus. Today is about battle tactics. From what I read in the guide book, we should focus on a simple, uncomplicated plan to ensure thorough understanding. I say the plan should be to get to the other side of the forest. That's pretty simple, right?" he asks.

Oh man, this is going to be harder than I thought. I knew I should have read that stupid manual.

"First things first," Kayla interjects. "We need unity of command. I'm commander for this mission. They'll have the element of surprise since we're in their territory, but if we stay together and focus, we can contend with whatever they throw at us." She continues, "Trion and I have been through these woods before. We've never made it all the way through, but it seems like the quickest path to the other side is to head north," she pauses to adjust her boot. "I'd say our five minutes are about up, so let's head that way. If it's the right direction then there'll probably be weapons for us to pick up along the way."

I'm not sure if Kayla's ability to control animals stems to people as well, but Trion and I begin moving north without question. The forest has a damp feel to it, as if it rained overnight. The leaves glisten with leftover moisture and the ground is soft under my feet. This is going to make us easy to track. I look down and sure enough, there are three sets of footprints leading into the forest. I try to lighten my step, but it doesn't have much of an affect. Hopefully, the ground will be firmer as we make our way into the center of the forest where the trees offer more protection from the elements. We're easy enough targets without leaving a trail behind us.

The sound of an arrow piercing a nearby tree stops us in our tracks. "Find cover!" Kayla yells.

We each run to the closest form of protection we can find. Kayla ducks behind a tree, Trion conceals himself behind a large stump, and I find a pile of fallen branches to hide behind. It's not much cover, but I'll take what I can get. Two more arrows fly at us, one narrowly missing Trion. This brings back some unpleasant memories from yesterday and I decide to let the others in on my theory about the arrows in case it can help us get through these woods. "I think they're using these arrows to control our direction through the forest!" I shout out.

"If that's true, they must want us to stop here. Everyone look around for weapons!" Kayla instructs.

We look around, but there are no weapons to be found and the arrows keep coming at us every four seconds. THUMP! One …two…three…THUMP! Then I see Trion do the strangest thing. He starts mumbling something under his breath and fully extends his arms out in front, shoulder width apart, with his palms facing out. He looks like he's pushing something away, but there's nothing there. I begin to feel a tingling sensation all over and my chest feels hot. An arrow flies at me a moment later. Just as the arrow is about one foot in front of my face, it starts to slow almost to a stop, which gives me enough time to roll out of the way.

"What was that?" I shout.

"I'm just running some interference!" shouts Trion in return. "I can't hold it for long though so we should get out of here!"

I get up to move and notice that my movements feel restrained, as though I'm walking through Jell-O. "Just push through it!" Trion shouts at me.

By the time I get a few yards away, I'm able to walk normally again. Kayla is already waiting for me. Trion backs away slowly from the scene while using all of his concentration to hold several arrows in their place. When he's far enough away he drops his hands, exhausted, and the arrows fall to the ground.

"Follow me!" Kayla commands and begins running north as planned. She's a fast runner and it's difficult for Trion and me to keep pace. We make it about five miles over the next hour or so before we have to stop, deciding to rest and go over our plan.

Kayla and Trion think we may have about forty miles of forest to trek through before reaching the other side. In order to make this distance before nightfall, we'll need to pick up our pace. Kayla suggests running in full-on sprints for short periods until we reach the end, but Trion and I don't think that strategy is going to work for our tired legs. While resting, I ask Trion about the "interference" he created earlier.

"Oh that," he replies. "That was just a simple spell I memorized. It allows me to slow the movement of objects or people within a close radius. It's an easy spell, but it's quite effective. I've memorized a few easy ones so far. Pretty cool, right?"

"Definitely – very cool." Trion's ability could work to our advantage. "What else can you do?" I ask.

"Let's see," he says, excited that someone has taken an interest in his skills. "I can also cast light, where I basically create light out of thin air. After I create it, I can manipulate it." A look of pride spreads across his face. "Oh yeah, I can manipulate light that already exists, too."

"You can manipulate light? What do you mean?"

"Yeah," he says. "You know, like I can use a spell to take the light from a room and make it into a concentrated form. It's pretty amazing. I can do all kinds of crazy stuff like turning light into a rope. I can even use it to melt things!"

I'm a bit concerned at this point about what sort of tricks Trion has up his sleeve, and if I should keep my eye on him.

It occurs to me that none of these spells will help us make it through the forest quickly, but at least we will be able to see if we get stuck here at night. According to Trion, the guide book warns of light creatures called Will-of-the-Wisps, which he says will try to lure us into danger at night. He says that with him around, we don't have to worry about them because we'll always have plenty of light. It's a small consolation, but it's better than nothing.

"OK, I think that's enough chatter. We're on a tight schedule guys," Kayla interrupts.

I have to tell myself to get up and keep moving because sitting here isn't getting us any closer to our goal. Not to mention that it makes us easy targets for whatever is waiting for us out here in these unfamiliar woods. We resume jogging, agreeing to keep a moderate pace to try to conserve our energy so that we all make it to the end. As we continue, I start to feel a tingling sensation again, which seems to be getting stronger. I look over at Trion, "What are you doing over there?" I say accusingly.

"Who me? I'm just jogging. Why, what's wrong?"

"Oh, um, nothing I guess."

And then I hear Kayla scream. She's a few steps ahead of us and is the first to sink. The ground around her appears normal, but with my next step I realize that it's not solid. I have just stepped into a quicksand-like matter. I soon find myself sucked into the ground along with Kayla. Trion, still several steps behind us, stops in time to avoid the trap.

"Hold on!" Trion cries. He tries to inch forward and grab me before I sink further, but he can't quite get close enough without the risk of falling in. He backs up carefully until he finds stable footing.

I'm close enough to the edge that I can grab ahold of solid ground and keep my head above the surface. I try to pull myself up a bit and flatten out on top of the muck to distribute my weight, but the dirt is forcefully pulling me down and it's difficult to keep from going under despite my grip. This is no normal quicksand. It's actively trying to swallow me. I look over at Kayla and she's almost completely consumed by the earth. The top of her head, from her nose up, is still sticking out of the muck and I can see the fear in her eyes start to set in.

I scan the surroundings. "Trion! Toss me that branch!" I yell, directing him to a large branch lying near the edge of the muck. Just when Trion picks up the branch, I see a little red cloth tied to the end. The realization that this was all planned hits me, and I'm furious. I take the branch from Trion, determined to get Kayla out alive. She sees me thrust it towards her, but she's unable to lift her arms from beneath the muddy, viscous earth. I have to force the branch under and hope that she can find it down there before disappearing completely. I feel a tug and begin pulling her towards me, but the weight of Kayla and the strain from the muck is too much. I hear a horrifying cracking sound as the branch starts to break.

Trion throws himself on the ground and sprawls out, anchoring his feet around a tree root and reaching his arms towards me. With one hand, I grab ahold of him and with the other I'm still trying to pull Kayla out to safety. With Trion's help, I manage to yank myself out of the muck and onto firm ground. Then with our combined strength, we heave Kayla out. She rolls onto the solid surface, coughing up brown, liquid dirt and gasping for air. Both of us are covered in muck.

"Thanks, Trion," I say, as I gasp for air. "And sorry I didn't thank you before for the arrows. I really owe you."

"No problem. We're a team, right?" he says as though this should be obvious to me.

"I guess we are," I reply. I haven't been a part of a team before – no sports or clubs or anything like that – and it's kind of a new concept for me. It's nice knowing that someone has my back.

We take a few minutes to rest so that Kayla can recover, and then we change our direction from due north to slightly east in order to avoid the quicksand-like trap. As we walk, the muck begins to dry and crack on my body. My skin starts feeling tighter. I hate the sensation, but maybe it will do something good for my skin like one of those fancy mud baths that Marion gets at the spa. There's always a silver lining. Derek taught me that.

I'm not so sure Kayla sees the silver lining like I do. She's been sulking ever since her fall into the muck. I think her ego is bruised more than anything and her sullen attitude reminds me of where I left things with my best friend. I will mend things with him first chance I get.

After walking and jogging for several miles, we arrive at the edge of a clearing, exhausted. I'm utterly joyful to see a small herd of horses grazing. They're exquisite creatures, all of them robust, powerful-looking animals.

"Now *this* I can handle. We'll be able to make it to the end of the forest in no time now," I exclaim and pick up my pace, heading straight for the horses. Kayla stops me with a swift tug on my right shoulder.

"Wait!" she whispers. "Could be a trap, Arden. How do we know we're not just being set up again?"

"Good point. How do you want to handle this?"

"Let me check it out. You two cover me in case something goes wrong."

Cover her with what? She strides ahead before I have a chance to ask.

Kayla enters the clearing, arms extended and palms up, as if to show she isn't armed. The horses nearest her pick up their ears, alerted to her presence, and stop grazing. A few let out agitated snorts. She makes eye contact with one and bows her head slightly, but never breaks her eye contact. To my amazement, the horse nods its head in return. She extends her hand and touches the horse on the tip of its nose. It sniffs her hands and then uses its muzzle to give her a light tap, as if to say "you're approved." The other horses relax their ears and begin grazing again. Kayla motions for us to come forward.

Trion and I enter the clearing. I'm way more excited than he is. I walk up to one of the horses and pet it gently. It accepts my gesture and seems at ease. Trion, however, does not seem at ease. He's crossed his legs and is wringing his hands like he's about to pee himself.

"Hey guys, what exactly are we planning to do with these horses?" he asks.

Kayla responds, "Ride them – duh. We'll make it in half the time with these beautiful animals helping us."

"About that, I don't have any idea how to ride a horse, let alone how to ride one barebacked."

"These are Arabian horses, Trion," I say. "Not only are they super-fast, but they're good-natured. You don't have anything to worry about. We couldn't have asked for any better."

"Oh relax, Trion, you can ride with me. I owe you," Kayla offers.

Kayla guides two stallions away from the herd and hands one over to me. I can barely contain my eagerness and after a few introductory pets, I hold onto the horse's dark mane and swing myself up. There is a renewed energy within me. The thrill of riding such a powerful animal registers deep in my soul.

Kayla hoists a nervous Trion onto a grey stallion and then swings herself atop. "Let's get out of here. We've got lots of ground to cover before nightfall."

We move swiftly through the forest; the horses' graceful power carrying us towards our goal with thundering hooves. The lack of padding seems to be getting to Trion though since he's grimacing a bit while trying to steady himself. I guess we aren't all equipped to ride these majestic creatures in such a natural state of being.

We're beginning to enjoy ourselves when, again, out of nowhere, an arrow comes zipping towards us. The anger, still leftover from our earlier disaster, boils up inside me, daring to rise to the surface. I've had it. I will *not* let them control me anymore. I turn my steed towards the direction of the arrows, yelling towards my teammates, "Sorry guys, but I'm going to have to take a detour!"

Kayla reverses the direction of her steed with ease, "Right behind you!" Trion almost slides off the horse from the sudden change in direction, but Kayla grabs him by his shirt before he falls off.

I race through the forest at a dizzying pace, no longer caring about the arrows flying past my head. The fury has clouded my brain and my only concern is finding whoever is shooting at us and making them pay. I weave through the trees with little effort, the forest proving to be an insignificant obstacle compared to my natural riding skills. My target seems to have caught on to my plan since the rain of arrows has lessened considerably.

Then I see her up ahead of me. A woman on a horse with a quiver full of arrows strapped to her back. She spots me and tries to make a break for it, but from behind me a stream of blue light shoots forward and wraps around both her and her horse, rendering them immobile. I feel a tingle shoot up my spine and warmth on my chest. When I look back, I see that the blue light is coming from Trion. His eyes are focused on the target ahead. My body is trembling from the rush of the chase and my growing anger. Without thinking, I ride up beside the stunned woman and jump from my horse, tackling her. I crash into her and we both tumble to the ground.

"What are you doing? Are you crazy?" she yells, still bound by the light, her voice strained and cracking from the weight of my body crushing her lungs.

"Am I crazy?! You've been trying to kill me for days!"

"I wasn't trying to kill you," she struggles to say.

"Oh really, well you could have fooled me!"

My anger is reaching a dangerous level now. I feel my cheeks getting hotter and I can practically see red. Then I look down at her face and my breath catches.

It's as though I'm looking into a mirror. I see the same disheveled chestnut hair pulled into a ponytail that I've seen every

day of my life; the same small, violet-blue eyes. Except it isn't my hair. These aren't my eyes. I pull back from shock and the blue light that's binding her slowly fades away. I allow her to sit up and as she does so, I notice a little glimmer of light about her neck. I look closer and see that the glimmer is coming from the sun catching on a gold chain. On the end of that gold chain is an exact replica of *my* talisman.

The woman locks her violet-blue eyes with mine and says in a disturbingly familiar alto tone, "Hello, Arden, I'm Dannia."

CHAPTER 8

Sisters

At first I can't focus. The red inside my head is so blindingly bright. I sit still, so very still, fearful of what I'll do if I allow myself to move.

"Listen, I know that this is a lot to handle, but I'm here to help you through your training," Dannia says to me. "I've been with you the whole time, even if you didn't know I was there."

"You were shooting arrows at me," I reply in a monotone voice. I stare into the face of this stranger, whose face is as familiar as my own, and I can't figure out if I want to punch her or hug her.

"Yes, but I was really just guiding you through the forest to help you tap into your gifts."

"But you're my sister! Your arrows *guided* me into a pit of giant man-eating bugs and caused my friends and me to almost drown!"

"Yes, I know, but you have to be placed in situations where you're forced to use your instincts, so that your natural abilities

surface. I was there the entire time and was ready to jump in if necessary. Trust me; you were never in any *real* jeopardy."

"Why did I have to tackle you before you introduced yourself? Why are we just meeting now? I thought you'd at least say 'hi' when I got here – you *are* my sister after all." I'm not letting her off that easy. I want answers.

"The Elders thought that my presence, any family presence, would disrupt your training. They felt that you needed to focus on the task at hand before any distractions were introduced. It's the same for all the Bravura. Believe me, I wanted to run to you as soon as I saw you – I had to stop myself more than once."

"So what happens now? I can't pretend that I haven't met you. There's no going back at this point."

"No, what's done is done. Truthfully, I'm glad that you caught me – even if it does mean punishment for me."

"Punishment? What'll happen to you?" I ask.

"It's alright. They'll probably just reduce my rations and make me do the grunt work at the training facility until they feel that I've made up for my infraction. Nothing I can't handle. Don't worry about it." She pauses, looking up at the sky, "It is starting to get late and you three haven't yet finished your mission. The least I can do is to show you the way to the other side of the forest. I know a shortcut."

I look back at Kayla and Trion. Kayla is standing staring at us with her fists balled up at her sides. Trion is tracing the dirt with the tip of his sandal and trying to look anywhere except at me and

Dannia. "This is your *sister*?" Kayla screeches. "She's the reason I almost died?"

"It's OK, Kayla, it was all just a part of training," Trion says, stumbling over his words in all of the excitement. "It's not her fault. Anyways, you heard her; it was all part of the plan. We were always safe."

"Speak for yourself! You're not the one who got caught in the trap! You're not covered from head to toe in the filth that almost killed you!"

"Well I know how you feel," I say. "And I get it if you don't trust her to bring us to the other side in one piece."

"We'll get there faster with her help, Kayla," Trion says and places a hand on her shoulder.

Kayla eyes up Dannia, gritting her teeth. "I guess we've got no other choice. We're not making it back in time otherwise."

"Alright big sister, show us the way," I say. Dannia gives a sideways glance at Kayla and then nods at me.

We mount our horses and Dannia takes the lead. She makes a hard right, bringing us in a new direction. I guess our navigation instincts need a little more honing. Too bad they don't have GPS devices in this realm. As we ride, I notice a gentle vibration coursing through my body. It feels like a shot of low voltage electricity. Not exactly the tingling sensation I had before, but something fainter, hardly detectable. I also notice that we're not being attacked. Nor are there any cleverly-hidden traps for us to fall into. With a clear path before us, it only takes about a half-hour before I see a break in the trees ahead and realize that we've reached our destination. Marcus is there waiting for us and behind him is the makeshift hospital tent.

Kayla is the first to dismount her horse and approach Marcus. "We've successfully completed our mission," she says.

"Yes, but not entirely through your own skills, I see," Marcus replies. He looks pretty perturbed.

Trion awkwardly dismounts from his seat behind Kayla, stumbling as his feet reach the ground. "Well that depends on how you look at it, Sir. Today was about battle tactics, and part of our strategy consisted of exploiting a breach in your security," he says puffing out his chest like a proud peacock until he looks over at me and notices the death stare I'm sending his way.

"Yes, we did have a bit of a *breach in our security*, didn't we, Dannia?"

"I can explain," Dannia says.

"Oh you will, but we'll have to save that for later. Right now we must make sure that these conquering heroes are cleaned up and well-rested before sending them on their way. Dannia, I trust you can take it from here."

"Yes, Sir, I'll make sure they're taken care of," Dannia replies.

She takes us into the hospital and on the way inside I see the two burly men and the young woman I overheard talking the other day.

"I recognize those three. I saw them yesterday in the hospital. Who are they?" I ask Dannia.

"They're Western soldiers who've been assigned to help prepare the Bravura here at the training camp. The camp's location is a highly guarded secret and only a few Westerners know where it is. It's an honor to be trusted with the secret," she explains.

"What's the big deal? It doesn't look like there's much here."

"Everything's here," she says. "Everything important, that is. The West has done a lot to protect the Bravura and the camp must remain a safe haven for those not yet ready for battle. It's how we're keeping our people alive. The East can't kill us all if they can't get to you."

"What do you mean? Why would the East need the Bravura to kill the West? And why aren't you one of the Bravura?"

"These are all really good questions, Arden, and it's good that you're looking for answers. You'll get the answers you need at camp through your training – in due time. For now, let's just get you cleaned up."

I decide to drop it for now, but I'm keeping my eyes wide open until I can figure out what's really going on here. Something's up, that's for sure. There's a reason why Dannia isn't telling me everything. I'm not a fan of secrets. People don't tend to hide good things from you.

Once inside the hospital, we're each brought to our own rooms. Inside my room, I find a tub of hot water and a sponge. Grateful for the chance to be clean again, I take the sponge and scrub the dirt from my body, trying to wash the memories of our near-death experience down the drain along with the muck. I begin removing layer upon layer of filth. The deep, rich smell of earth fills the room. The water turns a cloudy brown color, but I keep scrubbing until my skin is bright red. I want to make any last remnants of this horrific day – of almost watching someone die – disappear forever. No matter how hard I scrub though, I can't seem to rid myself of the filthy residue. It's like it's permanently stuck to my body, clogging my pores and stubbornly residing under my fingernails. I'm a mixture of red and brown.

I get out of the tub and put on the clean, cotton robe that Dannia laid out for me when she took my muddy clothes away to be cleaned. The soft feel of the cotton against my newly-scrubbed body is soothing. I decide to lie down in the cot and try to rest as the fatigue from the day overcomes my tired limbs.

I find myself back in the smoke once more, running for my life, the fear enveloping me. I'm so afraid. It feels like I know that I'm about to die. I continue clutching onto my bag like my life depends on it. Right on cue, my foot catches on the tree root and I begin tumbling.

I awake terrified as usual. Though this time, I find a new comfort when I open my weary eyes, the kind of comfort that only comes from family. Dannia is here. She practically leaps to the side of my cot, throwing her slender arms around me. "Are you alright? You were tossing and turning the whole time you were sleeping," she says, concerned.

"It's nothing, just the same old nightmare I have every night. Nothing new."

"The same dream… every night? What's it about?"

I go through my dream with her in detail. Too much detail if you ask me. Dannia asks a ton of questions and wants to know even the minutest aspects. Who knew my dreams were so interesting? By the time I reach the part about me tripping down the hill, she has an overly-concerned expression on her face.

"Don't worry about it," I say. "It's really not *that* scary."

"No, it's not that I'm worried about the dream itself. It's just well…have you been having any funny feelings lately?"

Funny? Like the funny feeling of living in some sort of twisted twilight zone being pulled back and forth between realms? Or maybe funny as in my new funny family dynamic where my siblings try to kill me? Somehow, I don't think that's what she means, so I just say, "I don't know, everything is a little odd lately. Why?"

"Well, reoccurring dreams tend to mean something here – if you're the right type of person."

"The right *type* of person? Like only AB positive blood types or something like that?"

"Yes, something like that. Listen, I know that you're scheduled to return to your home now, but I think this is something worth investigating further. I'm pretty sure that I can convince Marcus and the Elders to let us bend the rules and have you stay here a little longer… if you agree. We'll have to travel a little out of the way, but I think I know just the person who can help us get to the bottom of this."

"I'm down for a road trip," I reply. "I could use a break from training and I'd love to finally know what this stupid dream is about. Where are we headed?"

"How would you like to meet our father?"

CHAPTER 9

Road Trip

After lots of deliberation, Dannia is able to convince Marcus and the Elders at the training camp that we need to go see my father. I don't know why there is such a fuss over my nightmare, but I get the feeling that my lack of sleep isn't their primary concern.

Once rested, Kayla and Trion leave to go back to the Realm of Somnolence. Before they leave, I find out that Kayla is living in Miami with her guardian and Trion is in a group home somewhere in Philadelphia. Trion and I agree to make it a top priority to visit Kayla in the not-too-distant future, assuming we survive training and can get a few vacation days. Even the Bravura must get a vacay once in a while, right?

"We'll need to take a couple of days' worth of provisions to make it to father's house," Dannia tells me.

"A couple of days? Won't my guardians and Pax freak out if I don't come home soon?" Not to mention Derek – that is, if he's not too mad at me.

"Marion and Kenlin should be able to figure out that you're stuck in training," Dannia responds. She pauses and her face slackens, "Pax...the last time I saw him he was so small – just a baby," she says.

"He's huge now. Really... people think he's older than me," I say, like this is somehow going to make her feel better. She just smiles to herself.

We begin packing some bags that Marcus has given us for the journey. We take only the essentials – several containers of water, a couple loaves of bread, some apples, heavy woolen blankets, and a waterproof covering to use as a tent.

"If we hurry we should make it there in one day's time, but we need to be prepared just in case," Dannia says.

"No problem, as you've probably already figured out, I'm a fast rider," I respond, proud that I was able to catch her in training and ignoring the fact that she's most likely still stinging from it.

She brushes off my comment. "No, I'm afraid the horses won't dare follow us where we're going. We'll be travelling on foot."

Dannia leads us to a large flowing river and we follow it for about a mile or so until gradually our footsteps are deafened by the sound of rushing water. Moments later, we reach a clearing and I find myself looking up at one of the most breathtaking sites I've ever seen. It's a waterfall that's broken into three tiers. The crystal clear water flowing elegantly over each tier makes the falls resemble a fluid, sparkling veil. As beautiful as the falls look, the constant flow of water provides a powerful force. The mist from the spray blankets my body as we approach the falls, dampening my clothes.

We scale the rocks, which are slick from the spray, until we reach the second tier of the waterfall. The climb is hard, but it's nothing compared to the Adirondack Mountain trails back home that I'm used to. The sound from the falls is so loud that I know it's useless to try and ask Dannia where she's taking us. I follow silently, my senses overwhelmed by the beauty of it all. Suddenly and without warning, she dips behind the cascading water and disappears. I hesitate, not sure if I should follow, until I see a hand poke out of the water and wave me inside. As I pass behind the falls, I see that she's led us into a shallow cave-like formation located behind the water. It's cool and damp and it takes me a moment before I can find stable footing. Even though it's dark, Dannia moves through the cave with ease until she reaches what appears to be a dead end.

She places her hands on a stone at the base of the back wall and her lips begin to move, her voice muffled by the sound of the water. Blue light shoots out from where her hands and the rocks meet, spreading up the back wall like blue spidery veins. The wall begins to shimmer and then disappears, unveiling a deep, ominous tunnel behind it. Dannia waves me over and I clumsily make my way to the back of the cave to meet her. As we take our first steps onto the foreboding path before us, the blue veins of light flow ahead, climbing along the cave walls and cloaking them in pulsating light. The cave is both beautiful and eerie, and if I'm not mistaken, alive. I can't explain it, but I feel as though the cave is aware of our presence and could swallow us whole at any moment.

"Where *are* we?" I whisper, afraid my voice will awaken the tunnel.

"This is one of the paths out of the training camp. The camp is protected," she explains. "Unless you know the location of one of the passageways and the words to allow passage through it, you can't leave or enter. This way, intruders can't enter the camp. It also stops any daring Bravura from escaping into the outside realm should they locate an exit."

"That makes sense," I respond, pausing for a second. I think I've mustered up enough courage now to ask her what's really on my mind. "So...I was kinda hoping that you could tell me a little about mom and dad," I say hesitantly.

"Sure. What do you want to know? I can tell you most everything – just nothing war-related when it comes to them. Our father works on the highest priority tasks assigned by the Elders. Even I don't know all of the details."

"No, I don't want to know anything about the war. It's just...well, Marion and Kenlin say that the parents of the West had to give up the Bravura children to save them – that they didn't have a choice. But, I don't know... isn't there always a choice?"

"Marion and Kenlin are right," she responds. "Our parents were heartbroken when they sent you and Pax away. If there was another option, believe me, they would've chosen it. You have to understand that they did it for you – so that you and Pax would live. You'll come to understand that sometimes you have to do things you never thought you would for the good of your family...and for the good of your people. It's a reality of war."

"I know that they did it for us, but it just seems like it was so easy to give us up," I say. She just doesn't understand. How could she? She was the one who got to stay with our parents.

"Nothing about it was easy. Our parents were nearly destroyed from it. For a while, it was like I was an orphan left to fend for myself. Not to mention all the fighting that was going on at the time."

Dannia continues to tell me more about the fighting that took place between the East and the West and from what she tells me, she's fought in at least one horrific battle. Her voice is low and she begins speaking slowly, "I've tried to forget, but I can't. Their screams still ring through my ears. Each and every night I hear the voices of the dying crying out for my help. The cruel faces of the Eastern soldiers will forever be engrained in my mind."

"They toyed with us, Arden," she continues. "It was a game for them. If you were captured by an Easterner, you're greatest hope was to meet Death's friendly face as swiftly as possible, for if they decided they wanted to play with you first, agony would be your escort to Death's door. I've seen the East torture our people, cutting off one limb at a time, trying to get a Westerner to divulge a secret. 'Tell us where to find a Western Elder, and you might live,' they would say. Slice! First a finger. 'We'll spare your children and your wife if you tell us what we want to know.' Slice! This time an ear. It wouldn't matter though. They were always intent on killing every Westerner they could get their hands on, no matter what information they disclosed."

"I've seen one friend run his blade through another friend's heart just to save her from a crueler death at the hands of the East. Mercy killing it's called. But there is no mercy in war. There is only death. Sometimes I think it would have been easier to die in battle than to live with these memories."

After the battle, Dannia tells me that she was transferred to the camp to help train the Bravura and recuperate from the lasting effects of war. I never realized how hard this has been for my sister and it seems so silly that I was ever jealous of her. There were no winners in the decision our parents had to make, only different types of losers.

My feet start aching and it hits me that we've been walking for hours. I pull out an apple and take a bite. Its crisp juicy flesh washes throughout the inside of my mouth, answering the call of my growling belly and satisfying my hunger for the time being.

"It won't be much longer," Dannia promises. "My guess is that it's at least mid-day by now, which means that we should be reaching the end of the tunnel shortly."

Another couple of hours pass until finally the blue veins of light gather in an arch on a rock wall blocking our way. Again, Dannia walks to the rocks and places her hands on them. This time; however, she purposefully lowers her voice so that I can't hear. She must not trust me yet. The stones shimmer away, revealing a forest on the other side. We walk through the arch and the blue light flickers behind us, leaving nothing but rock. The forest that we've entered looks just like any other forest back at home, except for the trees. If it weren't for the turquoise leaves, I'd think we were in the woods behind my house.

"We need to hurry," Dannia says. "It's getting late and we don't want to be caught in these woods after dark."

We run until the outline of a village appears in the distance.

"Our father lives there, just up ahead. He's stationed there by the Western army to design artillery for the war. This village is one of the few remaining places that the East hasn't overtaken."

"Will he be expecting us?" I ask, feeling uncomfortable with the idea of sneak-attacking my dad with an impromptu reunion.

"No, but I'm sure that he won't mind the intrusion. Good old Potion Master of the Realm could probably use a break from all of his toiling."

"Potion Master, huh?"

"Yes, I nicknamed him that a while ago. I like to give him a hard time about his obsession with his work. It's just a joke."

"Must be nice to be so close."

"I'm sure you two will have your own jokes in time."

"Sure."

We quicken our steps until we reach our destination. The town is filled with old, stone buildings and winding cobblestone streets. It looks like it belongs in a European fairytale. I wouldn't be the least bit surprised to find a bunch of elves tucked away in one of these old shops making wooden shoes, or whatever it is that elves do. We appear to be in the center square, which is noisy and crowded. The streets are filled with people rushing home from a long day's work. At least that's my guess, since it's nearing suppertime and they seem only concerned with getting from point A to point B. People push past each other, shouting the occasional "Good day!" as they pass. The people are dressed simply. The men are in cotton trousers and shirts with plain leather moccasins on their feet. The women are wearing long dresses and most have shawls wrapped around their shoulders. The whole picture is decidedly outdated, and makes me long for a good pair of jeans and sneakers.

Dannia rushes me through the crowd, past the shops, trying to avoid being recognized. As we push through a crowd of people, I'm startled by a familiar face.

My heart skips a beat as our eyes meet. *Is that Zeke?* His gorgeous face somehow looks even more beautiful in this realm and I feel electrified upon seeing him. The contradictory knowledge that it can't possibly be Zeke and the concrete vision of him right in front of me is too much. The confusion of it all causes me to stumble, knocking down a woman in front of me and to my horror, causing a domino effect of crashing people. Before I can register what happened, Dannia yanks me into a side street away from the crowd and away from Zeke.

CHAPTER 10

Potions

"What are you doing? Are you trying to be seen? I promised Marcus we would get in and out of here unnoticed. If we get caught Marcus will have our heads!" Dannia scolds.

"I'm sorry. I was just surprised for a second. I thought I saw something." Me and my over-active imagination. Of course Zeke's not here. I need to stop daydreaming like a girl with a crush and start getting serious.

"Don't let it happen again," she orders. "We're here now anyway, so you shouldn't have a chance to cause anymore scenes."

We turn a corner and in front of us is a little shop covered in ivy with an apothecary sign in front. We cross the cobblestone street, being careful to avoid a passing horse carriage with an overeager driver. The sign on the door of the apothecary shop says closed, but we find it unlocked and walk in. The room inside is almost too small for the many potions and herbs contained within its walls. There is a large wooden table in the center of the room with a scale for measuring and a mortar and pestle for grinding. Hundreds of glass bottles and jars line the walls and each jar contains a different herb or colorful liquid. All are meticulously labeled. A puff of orange smoke from the back room causes us to cough. Someone from the back yells, "Who's there? Can't you read? The sign says closed!"

We walk through the back of the shop into the room where the smoke originated. I see a man. His back is turned to us. He's hovering over a contraption of intertwining tubes and jars. Purple and green colored liquids swirl around until finally meeting in an orange bubbly celebration in a jar at the base. "Aha! I got it!" The man exclaims and whips around to face us, jar in hand. When he sees us he drops the jar, causing a minor explosion and another large puff of orange smoke to fill the room.

"Dannia? What are you doing here? I wasn't expecting you for another month!" he manages between coughs.

"I know, but I brought someone with me who I think you'll want to meet."

The cloud of smoke starts to dispel. In front of me is an unassuming man with brown, unruly hair that is peppered with grey. He's dressed in long, dark brown robes. The lines by his eyes and the crinkle on his forehead are telltale signs of his years spent squinting above his experiments. Something registers inside when I look into his eyes and I know that the man standing before me is my father. He must know it too because his eyes tear up when he sees me and I know it's not just from smoke irritation.

"Arden," he says softly, as if he's afraid saying it any louder will cause me to vanish with the smoke.

"Dad?"

"Arden, my girl!" he exclaims and throws his arms around me. He squeezes me so tightly that I can barely breathe. His arms are strong. They are the strongest arms to ever exist and I feel safe within his embrace. I press my face into his chest and exhale fully until there is nothing left of me and I have vanished, lost inside his protection.

"How did you get here? They told me I couldn't see you until you completed your training."

"We need your help with something," Dannia interjects. I pull my head back and step away just a little, but my father keeps one arm around me. Dannia proceeds to describe my dream to my father, as he listens intently all the while.

"Well, well, this is indeed interesting," my dad says when she's finished. "I'm sure the Elders may see this dream as a possible threat," he says, almost as if to himself. "We must first; however, conduct a little experiment before we can know the true meaning of all of this." He walks over to a small desk at the back of the room and pulls a metal box from the drawer. He carries the box over to me.

"Please give me your bags and remove everything from your pockets," he says to me.

I hand over all of my traveling gear and the special bag Marcus gave me. I even give him a piece of stale chewing gum I apparently had stashed away in my camo pants.

"Eh em," he coughs. "I believe you have another item on your person?"

"Oh right, I almost forgot about this," I say, as I take off my talisman and hand it over to him. He places my talisman and the coin from my bag in the metal box and shuts it. He then asks Dannia to go into the other room with my bag. I'm starting to get a little nervous when he says, "The objective of this experiment is to determine whether or not you are a Sensitive, as I'm sure Dannia suspects. To do this, we must remove all magical items from your person so that your senses are uncontaminated. This metal box is made of lead and will confine all magical energy within it. Now, drink this potion and tell me how you feel," he says, handing me a vial of dazzling yellow liquid that he's pulled from a cabinet above his head.

I drink the bright liquid, trusting that my father means no harm. That trust is immediately violated. My head starts pounding and I can hear my heart beating in my ears as the blood rushes through my body. My skin tingles, so sensitive to touch that the clothes on my body agitate me. All of a sudden the light in the room is too bright and I have to shut my eyes. I hear a humming inside my head and my ears are throbbing. Then there's the smell. Even though the smoke cleared long ago, I can smell it now as if it just happened. A chalky, coal-like smell that makes me gag. I bend over in half and start to heave, my body in uncontrolled painful spasms as I vomit up what little food I ate on our journey. The acid in my throat burns ferociously and the sour taste it leaves behind makes me gag even more. Eventually, I'm able to pull myself up off the ground and open my eyes just a bit.

From the slits of my eyes, I see my father open the metal box and take out the gold coin. He moves the coin closer to my body. As it comes near me, the hairs on my arms begin to rise and my body feels on fire with the sensation of pins and needles poking into my skin. I can no longer hold in my agony. I let out a piercing cry. He takes the coin away in a hurry and slams the box shut. The next thing I know he's shoving another liquid down my throat. I reject the impulse to throw up and force it down. Once the liquid reaches my belly, a feeling of relief sweeps over me and the world around me returns to normal. My father scoops me up in his arms and lies me down on a plush couch. He calls Dannia back into the room.

"It is as you suspected," he says in hushed tones. "Arden is indeed a Sensitive."

"I thought so!" Dannia exclaims. "So what do you think the dream means?" she asks.

"Hold on," I say, still weak. "What do you mean I'm sensitive?"

"No, precious, not that you are sensitive," my father chuckles. "We're saying that you are a *Sensitive*. A Sensitive is someone who is able to detect aether, and can transmit and receive thoughts from others. You may also receive visions of events that are currently happening or will happen in the future. By having you drink that liquid, a special concoction of my own making, I was able to bring your senses to their full height. Your reaction once a magical object was introduced confirmed our suspicions. You see, only a Sensitive would react that way to magic."

Precious. I never thought such a little word could have such a huge impact on me. It's good to be with my dad again.

"So that's why everyone's interested in my dream, because it might actually happen?" I ask. "Exactly. Your dream may be a glimpse into events that will happen in the war. Any information that could give the West the upper hand is of utmost importance," Dannia explains.

"Or, it could just be a dream," my father says. "Only time will tell."

Awesome. Now I have to worry about that horrible dream coming true?

"Can you please explain to me what this aether thing is? I keep hearing this word and I have no idea what everyone's talking about," I complain.

Taking a seat next to me, my dad explains, "Aether is a resource that is found everywhere in nature. Think of it as a form of energy that can be harnessed and used by certain people to alter the state of reality." My confusion must be registering on my face. "To put it in more familiar terms, aether is the magic that wizards in our realm use to perform spells."

He continues, "The balance of aether in our realm is vital to its existence. It cannot be created nor destroyed, only used and recycled. That is why you cannot bring items from other realms into ours. Even the slightest changes could throw off the balance," he says, looking at my camo pants.

"Seriously? My pants are going to throw off the balance of your world?" *These people really need to lighten up when it comes to fashion.*

"It's your world too, Arden, and you never know what effect it could have."

"I think we'll just have to take our chances with that one," Dannia pipes in, laughing a little. "By the way, have you heard anything from mom?"

CHAPTER 11

Answers

My father sighs and says, "The last I heard from your mother she was stationed in Nautpolis near the Mystic Isles. I believe they were planning to head off some Eastern ships before they reach the shore. That was a few weeks ago though, and I'm expecting to hear from her any day now. Arden," he says turning to me, "I know that your mother will want to see you as soon as she can."

This seems like as good a time as any to bring up the burning question in my mind. It's the question that I've been longing to ask my parents my entire life and who knows when I'll get another chance. I take a deep breath and go for it, trying to draw upon all of my courage.

"Dad...why didn't you and mom come with us to the other realm? Didn't you want to be with us?" As soon as the last word escapes my lips, I wish I could take all of them back. My father looks as if I just ripped his heart out and stomped on it.

"Arden, if we could have come with you we would have. Believe me we tried. The Western leaders refused to let anyone valuable to the war efforts leave this realm. Being an alchemist, the weapons I create are vital to the West's survival, and your mother, the daughter of the Chief of the Hebelcaan, is a powerful huntress and warrior. Going with you would have meant treason and death for our family.

"We tried to give you the best guardians we could. We've known Kenlin and Marion for longer than I can remember and trusted them to watch over you like you were their own. Not every child from the West was as lucky as you two. Many were sent away in groups and have been raised by strangers."

His last words come out sounding a little defensive, which is understandable. I have a hard time feeling lucky about the fact that my father has been gone most of my life. It would have been nice to have him around on my first day at a new school or be there to give my winter formal date a lecture about bringing me home in time for curfew. You know, normal dad stuff that every other girl gets to experience. Still, I don't want to be the cause of any more hurt. "I'm sorry. I don't mean to sound ungrateful. It's just that I didn't realize that you even wanted to come back with us. Marion and Kenlin don't really talk about it."

"I'm not surprised they don't like to dig up old memories. Those were terrible days," he says with a sullenness that must come from years of carrying this burden.

"Could you tell me what happened?" I ask. "Please? I'm tired of not knowing the truth. Why are Pax and I different?"

"This is something that you're supposed to learn through your training, but I agree that you have the right to know the truth. All of this started a long time ago before you were born.

"You see, throughout the history of our realm, the Western Kingdoms and the Eastern Empire have been divided, kept apart by the Wall of Equiponderance. Both sides seemed to function peacefully and without conflict until Eastern warriors appeared one day on the Western side of the wall and began attacking the kingdoms without cause. The Western Kingdoms were taken off-guard and the East, moving as one succinct unit, was a force that the seven divided kingdoms of the West were not equipped to handle. Many of the Western territories were taken by the Empire.

"As the Western Kingdoms and Eastern Empire continued to wage war, the East started gaining more control. Eventually, the Western Kingdoms came together to form an alliance, known as the Alliance of the Seven Kingdoms. It was through this alliance that the West realized one very important commonality among the kingdoms – their children were disappearing at an alarming rate. One day they were here, the next day they were gone. And with each child that disappeared, the East seemed to grow stronger. What could these two seemingly separate facts have to do with one another? The answer was almost too obvious that we overlooked it at first. We didn't want to believe anyone was capable of so heinous an act.

"The reason the East was getting stronger as our children were disappearing is because each child that they stole had something in common. They were each born with a rare genetic trait that is found among the people of the West. Only a very small percentage of our people are born with it."

"So that's it? That's the reason? I'm some mutant that the East wants to steal?" I ask, starting to freak out.

"You're not a mutant, Arden. You were given a gift. You were born with an extra chamber in your heart – a fifth chamber. This chamber allows you to pull aether from the environment around you and store it inside. Once inside, it makes you more powerful than any normal wizard – should you choose to use the aether."

"So why don't the Bravura just use this against the East?" I ask. "If what you say is true, we should be stronger than them."

"The reason we don't do that is because if you choose to use your gift you will die. A body is not meant to house that much aether and it cannot withstand the strain. The East, however, doesn't care whether you live or die. It's their goal to capture you and turn you into a weapon against the West."

"Well I just won't do it. If they capture me…I just won't help them," I say defiantly.

"I wish it were that simple. If a Bravura is captured and they refuse to help, the East will rip out their hearts and use it to pull the aether themselves. It doesn't work as well or last as long as when a Bravura cooperates, but it does work.

"Now you see why the Western Kingdoms had to take drastic measures to protect their people. We decided that the only way to keep our children safe was to send them away. This was not an easy decision, but it seemed like our only option.

"And now, because of that decision, I've missed my children growing up. It's a sacrifice that no father should ever have to make. But, here you are, alive and well – perhaps the ends justify the means. I hope that someday you can understand why we did what we did."

I'm trying to digest all of this when a sickening thought hits me. "Dad," I say tentatively, "is there any chance that it could happen again? That the East could be kidnapping Bravura today?"

"Why, if that was happening…no…why do you ask?"

"I think I overheard something at the training camp about it."

"Dannia, do you know anything about this?" he asks my sister.

"I'm not privy to that kind of information," she responds, "but there's been some talk at camp about Bravura disappearing in battle. There's always rumors floating around. It's hard to tell how much of them are true."

"If this is true, then we're all in great danger," my father says. "We cannot let those dark days return."

Kayla and Trion's images flash in my head. Will they just disappear one day, kidnapped by the East? Do they even know what their fates could be? I suddenly feel the burden of this new knowledge. I don't know how, but I need to protect my friends.

My father pauses, drifting off momentarily before taking my hands in his, "Arden, how's Pax? Is he alright? Please tell me more about you, about your life. We have years of catching up to do."

Although I'm entirely disturbed, I get the impression that my father doesn't want to continue this conversation, so I cooperate and tell him about Pax. About how big and strong he's getting and how good he is with a bow. I explain what a natural he is with animals. I tell him that we're happy and have grown up well. I tell him anything to help ease the suffering that I know he must have gone through after giving us away. It's the least I can do.

Dannia is the first one to break the silence after I finish. "We really should be getting back now. Arden, you'll be able to go back to the Realm of Somnolence from here using your coin. I'll need to make my way back to the camp on foot come morning." She turns to our dad, "I'm sorry our visit is so short. I really wish we could stay longer."

My father's eyes start to glisten as he replies, "Oh honey, I'm just so thankful to see you both. You have no idea how happy you've made me today." And with that he hands me back my things, saving my talisman for last. He holds it for a second before handing it over. "You know, I made this for you, Arden, one for you and one for your sister. It has the symbol of your mother's tribe here," he says, running his hands over the gold work. "This is a very special necklace. I'm glad to see you wearing it."

"It's beautiful," I say, as I place it around my neck. "I never take it off. It reminds me of you and mom."

"It should remind you of your mother. It's beautiful and unique – just like she is, and just like you are. She would be touched to know that you think of her. I know that you and Pax are always in her thoughts."

I give my dad one last hug. After what my body has been put through, I'm not looking forward to the gut-wrenching transport that's about to take place. I figure the sooner I get it over with the better. I take my coin and say my goodbyes, not wanting to let my father or my sister go. This time, the tug from the coin reminds me that I'm being pulled away from so much more than just a foreign world.

CHAPTER 12

Car Trouble

The thought of going to school today is almost as painful as my crash landing on a pile of rocks near the old oak tree. Apparently, I wasn't picturing the *exact* spot that I wanted to go to clearly enough. Marcus the Mysterious could have warned me about the need for precision when it comes to magical transport.

I brush myself off, give the old tree a friendly pat hello, and hurry home. It's still dark out, so I figure I must have at least a few hours before I need to get up for school. I sneak into the house and stealthily make my way to my bedroom. The feel of my own bed is not just physically comforting; it's a perfect, long-awaited homecoming. My blanket is like an old friend wrapping itself around my weary body. I give in to my talisman disorder and wrap my fingers around my necklace before closing my eyes.

After my typical restless sleep, the feel of Sasha's tongue on my face is what wakes me up. There's nothing like a good coating of

dog slobber in the morning to get rid of the bags under your eyes. I gently push her head away to get her to stop licking me. I sit up and see that Pax is sitting on my bed staring at me. It looks like he's been crying.

"What's wrong, Paxy?"

"I thought something happened to you when you didn't come back yesterday. I was worried that you were hurt or something," he says.

It's nice to know that at least one of my siblings cares whether or not I get hurt, although his worries are a little too legitimate for my liking. "I'm sorry, Pax. Don't worry about me, I'm fine. They just sent me on a little field trip as part of my training. I do have some good news though. I met our sister at training camp and then she took me to visit dad," I say, hoping the news will cheer him up.

It works, because he immediately perks up. "What were they like? Did they ask about me? Did you meet mom too?"

"They were…interesting. They were both really happy to see me and wanted to know all about you. I can tell they miss you, Pax." This last sentence really seems to do the trick. Pax is smiling now.

"And mom? What's she like?"

"I didn't get to meet her yet because she's off fighting in the war. Dad hears from her sometimes. Hopefully, I'll get to meet her soon."

Just then Marion and Kenlin bust through my door. "You're back!" Marion shouts, while Kenlin scans the room as if tiny

enemies might be hiding in my pillows. "What happened to you? Were you taken hostage?" Kenlin asks.

"Uh, no. I wasn't taken hostage, Kenlin," I say, seriously questioning his sanity at the moment. "I just went on a little trip. I'm totally fine."

I can see both of their bodies relax and Kenlin lets out a big sigh of relief. Marion promises to make Pax and me chocolate chip pancakes for breakfast – a special treat in honor of me not being taken as a hostage.

Pax grills me for more details about our family. I tell him all about our sister's remarkable accuracy with arrows and our father's extraordinary way with potions. I leave out the part how I thought they were both trying to kill me at one point and how we have mutant hearts that the East would like to rip out of our bodies – no need to cause unnecessary anxiety. After he has had his fill, Pax takes Sasha downstairs to eat.

While I'm getting dressed for school, I can't stop my mind from going back to that moment in the village when I saw Zeke – or somebody I thought was Zeke. I hate to admit it, but even with all of these other things going on I still can't stop thinking about him. There's just something about Zeke that has burned his image into my mind, which has to be why I'm literally seeing him everywhere now. I have to say that the thought of seeing him at school today gives me butterflies. The kind that makes your heart race and your stomach do flip flops. I just know that this guy is going to be bad news for me.

After pancakes, I not only grab my school bag, but I also decide to take the bag that Marcus gave me. Today I've set the lofty goal of studying my guide book, which I'm praying is more interesting than History.

My legs feel shaky when the time comes to go to Derek's. I'm resolved to make things better with him, but the last time we spoke it was mostly me doing the talking and he didn't give any inclination that he was going to make up with me anytime soon. I'm not sure what to expect. Despite my fears, I will my feet forward to go meet Derek at his car. I start by taking slow, cautious steps towards the direction of his house, but my anxiety washes away the moment I see his face and I pick up my pace to a happy trot. I can tell that he's glad to see me.

We both get into the car, but Derek hesitates before putting the key in the car's ignition. He looks down at the keys in his hand, before turning to me.

"You didn't skip school yesterday because you were upset with me did you?" he blurts out.

"No, definitely not! I mean I'm not mad at all. Are you?" I can't believe he thought *I* was mad at *him* – like I could ever be angry with him.

"No way!" he says. "Well… not anymore. I was, but then I thought that I may have hurt you by acting that way and… anyway… you have *no* idea how much I missed you."

"I missed you too, Derek," I say, grateful to have my friend back. "I don't like fighting with you. Let's not do it again, deal?"

"Deal."

I wish I could tell him everything, just let it all come spilling out. It's killing me to have to keep such a huge secret from Derek. *What would he think if he knew about this other side to me?*

We start our drive to school, both of us in a better mood. Our improved cheerfulness; however, is short-lived. Soon after we leave, the sound of the car dying puts an end to our temporary joy and we're left stranded on the side of the road beside a cow pasture. The cows are unhappy that we've infringed upon their otherwise peaceful morning, and a couple of them let out disgruntled moos before walking away. Derek, determined to show off his manly car-fixing skills, refuses to call for help. He has his head in the hood of the car trying to figure out how to fix it when a shiny new black BMW pulls up beside us. The passenger window slides down to reveal Zeke and Cici looking impeccably polished and as well-groomed as ever.

Yep, there go the butterflies again.

"Looks like you're having a rough morning," Zeke calls from the driver's side. "Need some help?"

I can't see Derek from where I'm sitting. The hood of the car is blocking my view, but I can imagine what he must look like.

"No thanks, I've got this," Derek replies sharply.

The smirk on Cici's face makes me ball up my fists in rage, but I take a couple of deep breaths and somehow find my Zen.

"It's no problem. Why don't I take a look?" Zeke says more to me this time than to Derek.

I shrug my shoulders from inside the car, not able to speak, and hoping to stay out of the line of fire.

Zeke gets out of his shiny car in one swift movement, his Prada loafers barely touching the ground, and pops his head under the hood beside Derek. "Hmm, well it looks like it could be your alternator belt," he says. "I suggest calling a tow truck. I can give you guys a ride to school in the meantime."

"No, thanks, we're fine," Derek replies, with a touch of anger in his voice. "How do you know what's wrong with the car? No offense, but you don't look like you know a lot about cars."

"Oh none taken," Zeke says, sounding overly sincere. "Besides, if we judged people based on looks alone then where would that leave you?"

Derek slams the hood of the car down and scowls at Zeke.

"And I wasn't just asking you," Zeke continues and takes a few graceful steps over to my window. "Would you like a ride to school, Arden?"

I can feel my cheeks flush. "Uh, yes, please. Derek and I would both like a ride if it isn't too much trouble."

"It's no trouble at all. In fact it would be my pleasure," Zeke replies. This time he sounds earnest, which I think angers Derek even more.

I know that this will bother Derek, but I don't see any other option. He's just going to have to suck it up. I take both of my bags from the front seat and head over to Derek. "Look, let's just go to school and call a tow truck. We can pick the car up after school," I say.

"Fine, but I don't think there's anything wrong with the Honda. She just needs to cool off."

"She's not the only one that needs to cool off," I mutter under my breath.

"I heard that," Derek retorts.

I take a reluctant Derek over to our unlikely saviors and get in the back seat.

"That's a really nice bag," Cici says to me as I get in.

"This thing?" I say, pointing to my beat-up, nearly-as-old-as-I-am school bag.

She lets out an amused laugh. "No, I meant the other one. It's very unique. Wherever did you find it?"

"It was a gift from a friend." This is sort of true, which is good because I don't feel the need to add it to the growing list of lies I've been telling lately.

Zeke looks over to see what we're talking about and his eyes light up. Maybe Marcus has better fashion sense than I thought.

The ride to school is filled with awkward silence until Cici finally puts an end to it. "So, Arden, I noticed that you missed school

yesterday. Were you not feeling well or were you just playing hooky?"

"I think I came down with a 24-hour flu bug. I feel much better now," I explain.

"Glad to hear that you feel better. I know that Zeke and I both noticed your absence."

Zeke glances back at me with his beautifully intense eyes. "Yes, I definitely missed you in History. You were right. Mr. Gerber's hard to take. I could use your help in there."

"I'll be there today, so no worries," I say, pleased at the thought of him noticing my absence.

Derek looks over to me for a split second and I give him a *what am I supposed to say?* kind of look. I feel like I've just been caught doing something wrong – like I was sneaking a cookie before dinner or something.

I think that we're all relieved when we arrive at school and are no longer forced to be in such close quarters. Another mile or two and I may have been in the second car accident of the day. Only this time it would be from Derek strangling Zeke from the back seat. I could tell this was *not* Derek's idea of a good morning. I didn't mind it so much.

It hits me that Zeke and I have first period together, which means that he's probably expecting us to walk to class. I'm rapidly getting nervous about what in the world we're going to talk about.

Derek walks off alone as he gets out of the car, occupied with dialing a tow truck. Cici flitters off with some of her newfound girlfriends, which leaves only Zeke and me. Just as I had suspected, he says, "Do you want some company on the way to first period?"

"Sure, uh, yeah," I stammer, "that would be great." Awesome, I'm already off to a fabulous start.

Since I can't think of anything clever to say I decide to say something honest. "That was really nice of you this morning. I mean, you didn't have to stop for us. I don't think most people would've."

"I think you're giving me too much credit. I saw someone in need, so I stopped. To be honest, I was pleasantly surprised when I saw that it was you who needed the rescuing. I mean, I could do without Derek, and I'm not glad your car broke down... but still," he says with a half-grin.

"Don't mind Derek. He didn't mean anything. And you did kind of rescue us this morning, so I guess that makes you my hero." I cringe after this last sentence leaves my lips. It sounded *way* less cheesy in my head. To my relief, Zeke doesn't seem to notice.

"I'm definitely *not* a hero, Arden. You don't know me."

"I know that you'll stop for someone who needs help."

"Yeah, just like I know that you'll risk a beat down to protect someone weaker than you," he replies.

Oh great, he must be referring to that incident with the freshman kid. I *knew* he was watching.

"I must've looked like such a loud mouth," I say, embarrassed at my boldness.

"Not at all. You looked like someone who cares. You really surprised me that day."

I'm full-on blushing now and I can feel my heart start to race. I seem to be finding myself in this condition more and more when I'm around Zeke.

"You surprised me today when you took the time to help out a stranger. Seriously, thank you so much. I don't care what you say. You definitely *are* my hero today," I say surprised at how flirtatious I sound.

I see a flash of anger in his eyes. "You don't know what you're saying, Arden. You just need to stop," he says, his voice serious, almost threatening.

I feel a jolt of realization. He doesn't like me. Not in *that* way. I knew Emily was crazy to think Zeke could possibly be interested in me.

I try to save face by clarifying. "I didn't mean anything by it, just that you're a good guy."

"Exactly my point," he says as he looks directly in my eyes. His penetrating gaze pierces me to my core. "You don't know me, Arden, and you shouldn't be so quick to judge someone you just met."

I feel the tears well up in my eyes, my emotions starting to betray me.

"I just wanted to thank you. You know, it's OK to let people acknowledge when you do something good," I reply, my voice wavering.

His voice softens, "Once people think that you're good, then they have certain expectations of you… and then, it's incredibly easy to disappoint them."

I look up into his gorgeous green eyes and with all of my nerve say, "I doubt that anyone could find you disappointing." Then I push my way ahead of him and head into class so that I don't have to look him in the face.

I manage to make it to class and slide into my seat without letting a single tear slip out, still shaken by the conversation. I don't usually let myself cry and there's no way I'm going to let this guy get to me *that* much.

I have no idea what Mr. Gerber is talking about the entire class. All I can think about is how stupid I was for entertaining the idea that Zeke might like me and how I let my silly crush on him get the best of me. He must think I'm an idiot. I know that I do.

During class I try not to look at Zeke even though I desperately want to. I can see from the corner of my eye that he looks over at me several times, but my stubbornness wins out and I refuse to meet his gaze. I will not give him the satisfaction. I've already humiliated myself enough for one day.

I'm more than ready to go when the bell rings. As I start to get up out of my seat, Zeke pushes his chair over, blocking my way.

His voice is low and urgent, "Listen, Arden, I need you to do something for me."

"What could you possibly need from me?" I ask, my bruised ego showing in my voice.

"I need you to meet me after school today by the benches out back. Do you know what area I mean?"

"Yes," I say, a little uncomfortable with the idea of meeting Zeke at mine and Derek's spot. "I know the spot. Why do you want to meet there?"

"I just want to talk to you. I have something I need to tell you."

The next round of kids start filing in the classroom for second period, so Zeke moves his chair back to its original location and we both get up to leave.

"One more thing," he says pointing to the bag Marcus gave me. "I don't suggest carrying around things like that anymore."

"I thought you liked this bag," I respond, confused.

He looks at me like I've lost my mind and says, "Right… just don't do it again. OK?" and hurries out of the room.

My morning classes seem to move at a snail's pace and all I can think about is what Zeke wants to say to me. Does he want to apologize for being so harsh to me for no reason? Could it be that maybe he does have a crush on me too? Or, and I barely let this thought enter my mind, does it have something to do with the village yesterday in the other realm? Could it be that he *was* there and I'm not losing my mind? If he was there, then that would mean that he too is one of the Bravura and maybe he wants to talk to me about it. That would explain the comment about my bag and why he was so quick to notice my absence. Maybe he's going through this crazy experience too! I play around with the idea in my head. I could use someone to talk to, even if it is a guy I just totally embarrassed myself in front of.

It rains during lunch, so my typical lunchtime rendezvous with Derek is cancelled and we're forced to eat in the cafeteria. We find a table with Emily and a couple of other kids we know from classes. Emily is still all abuzz about Zeke, but when she tries to ask me about it I turn the tables by asking her about her favorite topic of conversation – Ryan.

"Have you talked to Ryan recently?" I ask, pretending like I don't know that they're in a mega-fight.

"No," she sighs exasperatedly. "I am *so* over him Arden! I mean who does he think he is anyway? If he thinks I'm just going to sit around twiddling my thumbs waiting for him to come back, then he has another think coming. I actually have a date tonight…and *not* with him!"

She goes into absurd detail about how he hasn't returned her phone calls or texts, and how she thinks he may be talking to this other girl from her gym class since she saw them together by his locker yesterday. After a minute or so of this she's forgotten all about me and Zeke.

Understandably, Derek is zoned out for most of the conversation, but eventually I get his attention while Emily continues on about Ryan to the rest of the group.

"Any updates on the car situation?" I ask.

"Poor old Betsy was towed to an auto shop down the block," he answers.

"Do they have any idea what was wrong?"

"Yeah, uh… the mechanic said that the alternator belt needed to be replaced," he mumbles in a barely audible voice.

I look away so that he doesn't see me laugh, but he catches me. He quickly joins in, releasing one of his dazzling smiles. It feels so good to have the old Derek back – the guy that's always there to laugh with me even at the smallest things. I don't think I'll be able to make it through this training without his smiles.

Later on, I finally have some luck in Mr. Stein's calculus class when my partner and I are the first ones in class to complete the timed assignment, with fifteen minutes to spare. Maybe things are starting to turn around for me. I begin to let go of my earlier hurt feelings, and I think that I'm ready to hear what Zeke has to say, no matter what he wants to talk about.

When it comes time to meet him in the back of the school; however, I see that he's gone MIA. No Zeke. Just my old familiar bench. I sit down at the bench and run my fingers over some of the various proclamations of love that have been carved into its weather-beaten wood. "Matt + Kim 4eva," "Tim loves Bailey," each couple enclosed in a perfectly shaped heart. *Maybe he's running late?* I look at my watch and see that class ended 10 minutes ago, so he should be here by now. He must have chickened out. He was probably just going to reiterate that he isn't into me and tell me he has a girlfriend back in Jersey. Looks like I got myself all worked up for nothing. That's just fine with me. He can have it his way.

I hurry over to the parking lot hoping that I can still catch a ride home. Derek texted me earlier that his dad was taking him to the auto body shop to pick up his car, so I know that I'm going to have to find my own way home. I'm happy to see that Emily is still there chatting away by her car. I take a quick glance around the parking lot looking for the shiny black BMW, but it's nowhere to be seen. Emily agrees to take me home and her girl-talk ends up being a good change of pace. It's hard to worry about anything when you have important things to discuss like whether or not Emily should wear her super-cute new skirt out on her date tonight.

When she drops me off, Derek's still not home yet, so I go straight inside. Marion is already making a big pot of turkey chili for dinner and Pax is sitting at the table doing homework. I sit beside him. It's nice to do something normal together after everything I've been through. The chili tastes especially good tonight and I appreciate the fact that no one is asking me questions about my journey yesterday. Pax gave them the rundown when I wasn't around and I guess they decided to give me a break for the night.

After we finish eating, I help Marion clear the dishes from the table and then go change into what I now affectionately refer to as my warrior chick outfit. I flit down the stairs and say "See ya later" to Marion, Kenlin, and Pax, trying to sound as casual as possible since I don't want them to worry. Before leaving, I make a special promise to Pax that I'll come back. I think he's still shaken up from my disappearance the other day and may need some extra reassurance.

I walk out the door towards the forest. A big part of me wishes that I could stay a little longer in my home. I know everything about this place and it's as comfortable to me as my favorite old pair of sneakers. This new realm is still strange to me. I know that it's supposed to be my new home, but truth be told, there's still too much of myself here in this realm to let another take its place.

A couple of steps out the door and I hear "Hey, AJ! Wait up!" I look towards the sound and see Derek jogging towards me. He stops abruptly when he sees me. "Nice get-up. Are you going for a new look?"

"Ha, ha," I reply.

"Listen, I didn't get to see you after school today, so I thought I'd stop by. I mean I figured you'd be missing me by now," he says, all grins.

"Yeah, yeah… so how's the car doing? Is she all fixed-up?"

"Oh, she's fine – running like new now. That's not what I wanted to talk about."

"OK, what's up? I'm in kind of a hurry."

"Well then, if you're in a hurry, I guess I better just get to it," he says a little mockingly.

I roll my eyes, "OK…"

His face turns instantly serious, "Look, AJ, there's something that I need to give you. I just can't wait any longer."

And then he cups my cheeks between his hands and pulls my face close to his until our lips meet. He kisses me softly, gently, as if he's afraid I might break. Something inside me stirs.

CHAPTER 13

Easterners

I'm first to pull away. Slightly stunned, I can see that he's waiting for me to say something. All I can get out at first is "Oh." How poetic. Uncertain of what my next move should be, I just say, "I'll talk to you later," and dash off into the woods. Derek probably thinks he just kissed a psycho with an affinity for buckskin, but I don't have time to worry about that right now. I don't even have time to worry about what *I'm* thinking right now. The sun is starting to set and I have a new mission in mind – to get to the Realm of the Awakened and find some way to see my mom. I push down whatever feelings I may have about Derek for the moment and concentrate on my new undertaking.

I use my coin and land in the field at the training camp expecting to see my sister and maybe Marcus the Mysterious, but instead I see Kayla and Trion waiting for me. They look worried. I can see that they have something to tell me, but neither one of them is making any moves. All my focus goes right out the window – so much for resolve. "OK, spit it out guys," I say.

Kayla accepts the challenge. "I don't know how to say this, but Marcus received a message from your dad... your mom's been injured in battle. He's waiting for you at his shop so you guys can go find her. Your sister never came back. We think she's waiting for you there too."

"Wh...what? My mom's hurt? How bad is it? Where is she? "

"Arden," Trion interrupts, "we don't know anything else. We only got here a little before you did. Marcus wants us to go with you, so you don't travel alone. He's off making the arrangements now."

The phrase, *be careful what you wish for*, flashes through my brain. Maybe I should have put some limitations on my wish to see my mother.

Kayla puts her hand on my shoulder, "It'll be OK, Arden. Trion and I are with you and we'll get you to your dad's in no time. Those Eastern creeps are gonna have to pay for this. I guarantee you that."

Trion pats me on the back. "I'll help any way I can. Don't worry."

The shock of the news strikes deep within. I have yet to see her again and she's already slipping away from me, along with the vague memories that linger in my mind. They're all I have left of her besides a simple gold necklace. I can't stand the thought of my mother injured. It might as well be me.

Marcus had instructed Kayla and Trion to wait with me in the clearing, so we find a soft patch of grass and rest while waiting for him to show. The sun is shining down on us, warming the earth. The sky above is a brilliant clear blue. If it weren't for the news I just received I would think this had the makings of a perfect day. Today is anything but perfect.

While we're waiting, I notice that I feel a slight vibration while lying next to Trion as he practices making little blue lights appear out of thin air.

"Hey, Trion, you're up to speed on your magical know-how, right?" I ask.

"I guess you could say that. I did read the entire guide book and I do know quite a bit for someone so new," he responds.

Kayla chuckles and shakes her head.

"Well, I've noticed that I'm feeling these strange vibrations every so often and I was wondering if you knew why."

"It could be a number of things. Do you have an idea yet about what your abilities are in this realm?" he asks.

"Actually, yeah. My dad said that I'm a Sensitive." Then I tell them about the trip to my see my dad and the crazy experiment he conducted on me only to figure out that I'm super sensitive (as if I wasn't already aware of that).

"No way! I've never met a Sensitive before – they're very rare. Like *really* rare. That means that the tingling you're feeling is your body's way of telling you that magic is near. That can be a very useful skill," he says. He seems impressed by me all of a sudden, like my stock just went up in his eyes.

I decide not to tell Kayla and Trion about our hearts – about the fifth chamber. I don't want to betray my father's trust and I don't want them to freak out. I'm sure they'll find out soon enough through training.

Marcus arrives with all of the supplies we'll need for our journey. In fact I would say he's given us more provisions than we could ever need. I mean, does he really think that we need to take along a 30 lb. battle axe? We all agree that the answer is no and, to Marcus's dismay, leave the axe behind. Marcus says that he'll accompany us out of the training camp since he's the only one of us who knows the password to leave and he's not willing to divulge this secret. Then, once I make it safely to my dad's shop, Kayla and Trion are to use their coins to come back to the camp. The plan sounds simple enough.

We begin our journey through the forest. All the while Trion rattles on about the wonders of magic and how alchemists, like my father, are more science-oriented and tend to think that magic is all a bunch of "hocus pocus." He tells me that he's sure my dad is a great guy though, even if he is an alchemist, which I gather I am supposed to think is very big of him to say.

I'm thankful when the sound of the waterfall overpowers Trion's voice, although that doesn't stop him from talking.

Marcus leads us into the cave behind the falls, but we wind up needing to coax Kayla through the water since she does *not* enjoy getting wet. Once she's inside, I can tell that she thinks the journey was worth it. It really is amazingly beautiful and when Marcus opens the gate to the tunnel with the blue flowing lights, even I'm in awe despite having already seen it.

Inside the tunnel, we move at a rapid pace. I think that the adrenalin of the journey is pushing us forward. I need to get to my family as fast as possible, and Kayla and Trion have something to prove since this will be their first quest outside of the training camp.

There isn't much chatter during the next part of our trip. We're all focused on our mission and the gravity of the situation has set in. My mother is somewhere out there on a battlefield, injured, and she needs us – my father, my sister, and me. I have to make certain that I don't let them down, and Kayla and Trion are here, standing beside me, to make sure that I don't. For the first time, I'm beginning to realize what it means to be one of the Bravura. How it actually stands for something. If one of us is in need, then all of us are. Being part of the Bravura may mean bravery against all odds, but it also means that you're never alone in the face of danger. Our bravery comes not only from within, but from each other.

I can feel a change within, like I've gained a deeper understanding of myself and of my people. Or maybe it's that I've realized that there is no separation between us, that we're one and the same. I feel stronger now. I'll need this newfound strength to keep an eye on Kayla and Trion during this journey. There can't be any Bravura disappearing on this trip. Not on my watch.

We reach the end of the tunnel, breathless, but determined.

"This is where my part of the journey ends," Marcus says. "Move as quickly as possible and do not get deterred. Remember your lessons and stay out of trouble. I'll expect to see you back at camp soon. I would wish you good luck, but you don't need it – you are Bravura." And with that we watch him fizzle away behind us as we leave.

Without Dannia here, the forest seems much more intimidating. I'm starting to notice things that I didn't before. Like how I don't recognize some of the forest noises. I think back to my training with Kenlin and all of the animal sounds I've studied. Still, I can't place the noise coming from the trees. Maybe a monkey is causing the sound? A very disturbed, grossly unnatural monkey? Whatever it is, it wants us out of its forest.

"So which way are we headed?" Kayla asks me.

"Oh…um… I was so excited to be going to see my dad the last time that I didn't pay attention," I admit. "I think it's this way," I say pointing ahead of me.

"Seriously? Well what are we supposed to do now?" she asks.

I feel like I've greatly disappointed Kayla. She doesn't seem to understand that we aren't all born with her natural sense of direction. Trion is more forgiving and simply gets out his guide book to help us find the shortest path to the village.

About a half of a mile into our journey we hear voices nearby that bring us to a halt.

"Did you hear that?" Kayla asks.

"Sounded like two male voices," I reply.

"Take cover! No one make a sound!" she commands.

Kayla and I find cover easily enough behind some nearby bushes, but Trion is spotted tripping on a twig just before he can duck behind a tree.

"Hey! You there!" one of the men shouts.

From what I can see through the bushes, there are two men, both of them tall and muscular, and both are wearing the same purple and black clothing. They're carrying swords and look like they wouldn't hesitate to use them.

"I said, YOU, behind the tree, come out where I can see you!" the man shouts again.

Trion walks out from behind the tree, visibly shaking.

"What's the matter little feller?" the other man taunts. "Is there a reason you're so scared?"

"I'm not scared," Trion replies.

"Of course you aren't," the man mocks. "Are you travelling out here all alone?"

"Yes, I was just taking a walk through the forest," Trion shakily answers.

"Were you now? You know, these woods are off limits today – orders from the Eastern Emperor."

"I wasn't aware," Trion says, regaining some control over his voice.

"You weren't *aware*? You mean you weren't aware that you're trespassing?"

"No," Trion says, "I wasn't aware that these woods belong to the Eastern Emperor."

"Is that supposed to be funny? You Western scum! As of today, these woods are the property of the East and anyone who thinks differently will have to answer to us!"

I can feel my fear mounting as I watch Trion, a Bravura, standing right in front of the Eastern soldiers. If the soldiers find out what he is, will they try and capture him? I look over at Kayla thinking that we need to come up with a plan and fast, but I see that she's already beaten me to it. She's taken a rope out of one of the bags that Marcus gave us and is busy tying an intricate knot with her hands. I follow her lead and search through the bag. Inside I find a long, sinewy knife, the blade made of dark metal. It looks solid and menacing. I'm starting to regret the decision to get rid of the battle axe.

The men continue to approach Trion, snickering as they get closer.

Kayla turns to me, a look of understanding in her eyes, "Now!" she whispers.

We jump out simultaneously. I shout at the men to distract them, but before they have time to notice me, Kayla has already snared them with her rope. She looks at me, "Do it NOW, Arden!"

Aware of the knife in my hand, I comprehend what she wants me to do. I fly towards the men, the knife poised in my hand above my head ready to deliver their final sentence. At the last second I waver. Instead of sending them to their graves, I hit them each over the head with the hilt of my blade and they lose consciousness.

"Are you *kidding* me?" Kayla asks, flabbergasted at my inability to follow-through. "These are Eastern soldiers, Arden. And they know we're here. We can't just leave them."

"I know, I know, I just couldn't do it alright?" I reply.

"What are we supposed to do with them now?" she asks.

"We could tie them to a tree. We could use our rope and Trion can reinforce it with his binding spell, right?" I ask.

"No, sorry, it only works if my target is in my line of vision. As soon as we leave it'll wear off," Trion explains.

"Do you know any other spells that could help?" I ask, hoping that I can somehow rectify the situation I put us in.

"There *is* a paralysis spell, but I haven't practiced it yet, so I can't guarantee it'll work."

"It's worth a try. Give it your best shot, Trion," I say.

Trion takes out a piece of parchment from his bag. The paper is blank, but he appears to be reading something from it. He finishes reading and looks up at us for our approval.

"Well?" he asks.

"Well what? Nothing happened," I say.

"Hmm, well it says here that the only way to tell if it worked is if your target stops moving. These guys were already pretty stagnant, so I guess we can't know for sure."

"Fine," Kayla steps in. "We'll have to take our chances. Let's tie them to a tree just in case. We should take their uniforms too. Not really a good idea to leave two tied up Eastern soldiers out in the open."

It takes all three of us to drag their heavy bodies to a tree that's far enough away from the path to keep them unnoticed for at least a little while.

After we finish tying the men up, we stuff their uniforms in our bags and try to hide the traces of the scuffle. As we continue our trek to town, Trion says to Kayla, "Where did you learn how to tie such a fancy knot?"

She replies, "My guardian taught me. She has a boat and we used to practice knots together whenever she took me out sailing."

"Sailing huh? I bet you loved that. All that water, the feel of the ocean spraying your face," Trion teases.

"Yeah well, you know, that whole situation we just went through back there would have been a lot easier if *somebody* had just used their binding spell to begin with," she retorts.

"I know. I'm not sure what happened. I just froze up."

"Don't worry about it, Trion," I say, patting him on the back. "This is new for all of us."

"That's easy to say coming from the girl who just tried to tap someone on the head to death," Kayla chimes in.

We walk in silence the rest of the way to the village.

Nighttime approaches rapidly. Our run-in with the soldiers has delayed us, and there are only a few more moments of waning sunlight before we'll be left in utter darkness. We take our first few steps on the winding cobblestone streets and I notice that something seems off about the village. Kayla says aloud what is just now running through my mind. "Where are all the people?"

"Maybe they're all indoors because it's getting late?" Trion offers.

"It's not that late, and besides, shouldn't there be at least *some* signs of life? Look around; there isn't even a window open or a light on. Was it like this before when you were here, Arden?"

"No, it was exactly the opposite. The streets were filled with people. It was earlier in the day though."

"Look, this can't be a good sign. Let's not walk out in the open anymore," Kayla suggests.

To be safe, we take to the shadows, hugging the sides of the stony buildings as we creep through the village. If anyone saw me doing this back home they'd assume I was about to rob them and call the cops on my creepy behind.

Then we see them. Three more Eastern soldiers patrolling the streets.

"Have any of you seen Frederick or Reginald? They were supposed to be back here over an hour ago. Frederick is supposed to be taking my place on this patrol. I have a nice hot leg of lamb waiting for me at home and I want to get back to it," one of the men complains.

"Oh you know Freddy and Reg, they're probably just passed out somewhere after hitting the bottle too hard."

They must be talking about our Eastern friends from the forest. Well, they have it partially right – good ole Freddy and Reg are undoubtedly passed out somewhere, I think to myself with a smirk. We wait in the shadows for the soldiers to pass. I have to hold my breath the whole time out of fear that I'll make a noise and draw their attention. Poor Trion is shaking again.

After the soldiers have passed and turned the corner down an adjacent street, we begin moving again, this time at double the pace. These streets aren't safe for us and I'm starting to fear for my father's and sister's safety. I stop myself before I let my fear take control. I can't let my mind entertain thoughts like that now. I must get to my family.

My knees buckle when I see the small apothecary shop and Trion has to catch me. The front door is completely unhinged, lying in broken pieces on the ground. The windows are shattered and the small apothecary sign is barely hanging by a single rope, crooked above the empty space where the door once stood.

"Everybody stay calm and move quietly. Someone could still be in there," Kayla whispers.

Yes, someone could be in there – like my father or my sister. I ignore her command and rush inside the store. The sound of the glass crunching beneath my feet brings me to a halt. The entire store has been torn apart, all of the pretty colored glass bottles now lying in ruins. Chemicals that shouldn't be mixing with one another have found each other on the floor, creating unnatural concoctions and adding a putrid smell to the place.

Kayla and Trion rush in behind me and stop when they see the inside of the store. I frantically look around the room, but no one is there. Maybe that's good I tell myself. At least they're not in a bloody heap on the floor. Then I remember the back room. Yes, maybe they are hiding somewhere in the back! My father probably has a hiding spot ready in case something like this happens.

I bust through the back door expecting to see my father and sister waiting for me, but what I find instead is so unexpected that I freeze. All I can do is stand there, mute. Kayla and Trion follow me inside, each drawing a knife as they approach. They too, are brought to a halt. "Who's he?" Kayla asks, confused by the expression on my face.

"Oh him?" I manage. "His name is Zeke."

CHAPTER 14

Deception

Sitting amongst the rubble in the room is Zeke, looking tired and uncharacteristically small amid all the wreckage. He looks up at me, "Listen, I can explain."

"Explain? Fine, go ahead and explain why you're sitting here in my father's shop that's been torn to pieces and why my father and sister are nowhere to be seen," I say.

"I came here to warn you, Arden."

"He's wearing an Eastern uniform!" Kayla interjects.

"Yes, but I'm here to help, I swear! Just give me a chance!"

"Arden, why are you just standing there? We should tie him down or something," Trion says.

"Wait, just let me explain!"

"Bind him, Trion," I say callously.

This time, Trion has no problems releasing the blue binding light on our prey. A tingling sensation flows through my body in response to the outflow of magic.

"Now, please *do* explain why you're here, Zeke," I say, as if challenging him to say the wrong thing.

He begins hurriedly, "Look, the Eastern army has known for some time that your father has been supplying firearms to the West, but they didn't know exactly where he was located until about a week ago. They've been planning an attack on the village since then. I tried to warn you about it yesterday when I asked you to meet me at the benches, but I wasn't able to make it to you."

"Yeah, I remember that," I say, a hint of resentment in my voice.

"The Eastern army came here yesterday to capture your father, Arden."

"What about my sister? Were they both taken?"

"I don't know. I never knew your sister was part of the plan."

"Why did you come here now? And why should I trust you? You're obviously working for the other side."

"I was, yes. That's why Cici and I were sent to your school. We knew that there were Bravura located in the area and to be honest, I knew it was you the first time I saw you. I could just feel it in my body. But you, Arden, were just so unexpected. I didn't think I would feel this way. I didn't think I even *could* feel this way about anyone. I wanted to…to protect you. From the moment I saw you, that's all I've wanted to do. I was hoping that I could keep you away from all of this," he says and looks at me pleadingly. "I promise that I didn't say anything to Cici. I wouldn't do that to you. Unfortunately, she was convinced you were the Bravura we were looking for when you brought that bag into school. As soon as my sister realized who you were, I knew that she wouldn't hesitate to carry out the rest of the plan. By then though, I couldn't do it. I couldn't hurt you like that. Not after I met you and saw for myself what kind of person you are. You have to believe me."

"Wait," I interrupt. "What are you talking about? What plan did you and Cici have?"

"Arden," he says, "…they have Pax."

The world around me stops. I can no longer hear what he's saying. His words just repeat over and over again in my head, *they have Pax.* Pax, my little brother who's never left the comfort of our home and the warmth and protection of Marion and Kenlin. He's must be scared out of his mind wondering where I am, wondering if I know that *they* have taken him. My heart breaks when I remember my last words to him. I promised him that I would come back.

Kayla shakes me to my senses. "Arden, it's a lie. He's trying to manipulate you. That's what they do. He's one of them, remember?"

"Is she right, Zeke? Is this all a lie?" I ask him.

"No, I swear, it's the truth."

For some reason I feel like he's telling the truth. Not that it matters. I have no choice but to take his word for it. If there's even the slightest chance that they have Pax, I have to try and rescue him.

"Arden," Zeke continues, "They only took Pax to get to you. They won't hurt him. They want you to tell them the location of the Bravura training camp and they're hoping to use Pax as a bargaining chip. That's why they sent Cici and me to your school. To find you and make you talk. I didn't even realize that this was your father's shop until I saw you in the village the other day. I figured coming back here would be my best chance of finding you."

It takes me a moment to process this information. I know that Zeke isn't telling me the whole truth. They didn't just take Pax to get to me. And I doubt that they'll just let us all go once we tell them what they want to know. No, they won't hesitate to rip our hearts out after they're through with us – that I'm pretty sure of. The only way out of this is to rescue Pax, assuming he's still alive.

"So, what now? What's your big plan?" I ask angrily.

"I'm hoping that you believe me and let me help you. I can show you the way to your brother and help you get him out."

"No way, this has to be a trap," Trion interjects.

"He's right, Arden, no way we can trust him. I say we tie him up and leave him here to rot," Kayla says.

I look into Zeke's eyes; those beautiful green eyes that once made my heart skip, and feel only disgust. I'm disgusted that he could be so cruel and manipulative, and disgusted at myself for falling for him. I can't just tie him up and leave him to die though. If he's telling me the truth then I need him to find Pax. Also – and maybe this is just my ego not wanting to admit when I'm wrong – part of me is still holding onto the idea that maybe he really is trying to help, that the good guy I thought I saw before is in there somewhere.

"No," I say. "I have no choice but to listen to him, even if I don't necessarily believe him."

"You're a fool then," Kayla replies.

"Maybe so, but if the Easterners have my brother, then I need Zeke to show me the way to him."

"Fine, but he'll just lead you to your death. Can't you see through this? You may have a death wish, Arden, but you aren't dragging me down with you," Kayla says.

"Enough, Kayla!" Trion shouts. "If Arden goes with this Easterner, then we're all going. We are the Bravura and we don't leave each other behind."

Kayla doesn't say anything in response this time. Instead she lets out an exasperated huff and storms out of the room.

Trion turns to Zeke. "I hope you know what you're doing, Easterner. If I find out that this is a trap, I'll make you wish that we did leave you here to die."

"OK, Zeke, where do we go from here?" I ask, not even trying to mask my hostility towards him.

"I know where they're taking Pax, but we have to hurry. This town is filled with Eastern soldiers now so our best chance is to get out of here while it's still dark."

Kayla reenters the room. "He's right. If we're planning on getting out of here alive then we need to make our move."

Trion gives Kayla a smile. She just glares at him in return.

"If we're going to leave here together, then can you please release these binds?" Zeke asks.

"Don't push it, Easterner!" Kayla yells.

"Fine, I guess I can't hold the bind the entire way anyway. But remember… I warned you," Trion says and lets the blue lights that are wrapped around Zeke's body sputter away.

"Where are we headed?" I ask Zeke.

"To the city of Wellsport. That's where they're taking Pax."

"Wellsport? How long of a journey is it from here?"

Trion adjusts his bag on his shoulder, "I could look it up on the map in our guide book…"

"Is that a good idea? We don't want this Easterner knowing what's in there do we?" Kayla whispers to Trion and me.

"Hey guys," Zeke interjects," you should know that we already know the Bravura carry books with them, so you don't need to be all secretive. Not that you three are very stealthy anyway. I'm pretty sure anyone walking by on the streets would've heard you talking just now."

"He did already know about my bag, so I'm not surprised he knows about our books. I don't see the harm in opening a map in front of him," I reason.

Trion takes out his book and flips it open to the map.

"Whoa, I didn't realize that the book was so big! That thing must be heavy," Zeke says, causing Kayla to give him a vicious scowl.

I peer over Trion's shoulder at the map and my breath catches. Wellsport is only a short distance from Nautpolis, where my mother was last stationed. Maybe she's still there! Maybe she really is injured and is waiting for my father and sister to arrive, not knowing that they have been captured and will never come to her aid. I can't know for sure if the message from my dad was real or if it was a ploy by the East to lure us to my dad's shop, but I'm going to have to find out. First though, we have to save Pax. After that, I'll need to find the rest of my family on my own. Kayla and Trion risking their lives to help me save Pax is one thing, but I'm not willing to let them do it again.

"It looks like Wellsport is a couple days journey from here on horseback. We won't get there for weeks if we travel on foot," Kayla says.

"Well then, I suggest we steal some horses," Zeke says.

"Oh do you? You think we should just walk right out there into streets that are teaming with Eastern soldiers and help ourselves to their horses?"

"Yes, that's exactly what I think we should do. If I'm not mistaken, that's an Eastern uniform you have poking out of your knapsack, right?"

Kayla hesitates, "Yes, it is…"

"How many of those do you have?" Zeke asks.

"Two, but there are three of us."

"Well, then, who wants to be my prisoner?"

"Excuse me! I think you're confused. You see *you* are *our* prisoner!" Kayla exclaims.

"I meant no offense. It's just that for all three of you to make it out of here alive, you'll have to disguise yourselves as Eastern soldiers. Since there are only two uniforms and three of you, one of you will need to act the part of a prisoner."

"I'll do it," Trion volunteers. "I'll be the prisoner."

"Trion, you don't have to do that," I say.

"No, it's the best way. It's more believable that you three caught me. I mean, look at me. I wouldn't pass for a soldier anyway."

"He's got a point," Kayla agrees.

"So it's settled. You two are now Eastern soldiers and you, Western wizard, are our prisoner," Zeke states.

"Uh, it's Trion."

"Of course it is."

Kayla and I grudgingly pull the uniforms from our bags and slip them on. They are much too big for us and hang loosely on our slender frames. The heavy cloth stinks of sweat and body odor and hasn't been washed in weeks. The uniforms come with hooded cloaks that we're able to pull over our heads to almost completely hide our faces. The transformation is complete. Shrouded in the stench of our enemy, the purple and black colors covering our bodies, we are now Eastern soldiers. Albeit not very convincing ones.

"That's not a bad look for you, Arden. Purple really brings out the color of your eyes," Zeke says in a hushed whisper under my hood.

I feel the rage swell up in my chest and I push him with both hands so that he stumbles backwards into a table full of the broken remnants of my father's potion bottles.

"Hey, relax. I was just playing," he says.

"Well it wasn't funny and this isn't a time for games. Let's just get this over with," I say, the anger emanating from my body.

"I fully agree," Zeke replies as he brushes the broken pieces of glass from his person. "Now, if you'll just follow my lead, I think I can manage. Four horses coming right up."

We follow Zeke out of the shop, careful not to step in any number of smoking chemical mixtures that have been stewing on the floor. As we walk through the gaping opening of the store, I feel a mixture of sadness and panic rush over me. What if I'm the only member of my family who hasn't been taken by the East? Or worse, did my father and sister meet their demise in this ruined shop? As hard as it is to not know for sure what happened, the uncertainty at least gives me reason to believe that there's a chance my family may still be alive. That little glimmer of hope is all I have left to keep me going at this point.

It goes against my instincts to walk right out into the open after all of the sneaking through the shadows, but Zeke assures us that we'll be OK as long as we do as he instructs. He says that he knows where there are some horses and it should be easy enough to get in and out without causing a commotion. I'm not comfortable with the idea of letting an Easterner lead us around blindly, but I go along with it. It's our only chance.

His plan seems to be working when we reach the stables without incident. The horses, resting in their stalls, are large, muscular creatures. They are completely black with purple plumes attached to their bridles, signifying that these poor animals are the property of the Eastern army.

We approach them cautiously, not wanting to cause a disturbance, and find that they're more docile than their looks would imply. We begin saddling three of the horses since Trion has respectfully declined the opportunity to have his own.

We're about to mount our steeds when two men come stumbling into the stable. "Hey! What do you think you're doing?! Those horses are meant for the night watch."

Zeke turns to face them. "Yes, well, there has been a change of plans. There are new orders now. We need them to take our prisoner to the High Court to stand trial for treason against the Emperor."

"Prisoner you say?" one of the men says while looking around the stables for the person in question.

He finds his target and I watch Trion's body tense as their eyes meet. After a moment I know why – these men are the soldiers from the woods. I feel my heart jump up into my throat as I realize that we're wearing their uniforms. I notice that they both have large, red welts on their heads. Guess I'm not too shabby with the hilt of a blade.

"Hey, I recognize you! You're that little wimp from the forest! Where are your friends now, little Westerner?"

"Yes, we found him running from the forest earlier this evening… alone," Zeke says.

"Is that so? How come you're the only one talking, eh? Who else do you have with you?"

Just then, Zeke pulls two small daggers from his boots and before I have time to register what's happening, he hurls them into the chests of the men. They fall back in surprise, grabbing at the blades, and choking on their own blood. Little red bubbles of salty liquid flow out of their mouths.

"Hurry, we have to get out of here before anyone else shows!" Zeke commands and retrieves his bloody daggers from the chests of the dead men.

We mount our horses – me, Zeke, and Kayla with Trion on her back – and ride as fast as we can from the stables until we reach the shady protection of the forest.

"What was *that*?" I ask Zeke, shocked from what I just witnessed, my hands trembling as I hold onto my horse.

"What? Would you rather that we were all captured and tortured for treason?" he asks.

"No, it's just I didn't know you could do that."

"It's like I told you before, Arden. You don't know me at all.

CHAPTER 15

War Stories

We continue riding until the sun reveals itself and the moon begins to fade. We've been travelling for what seems like days. Exhaustion has set in, and we need to rest. Marcus's over-preparation has come in handy since we find that he's packed us each a waterproof tent, blankets, and enough food to last a couple of days.

There's a chill in the air and because it's morning, we're less worried about the light of a fire drawing unwanted visitors. Kayla lays the groundwork by providing some twigs, kindling, and larger pieces of wood. Trion does the rest by using his light spell to start a spark. The warmth from the fire is calming after our long ride in the cold. Following a quick meal of dried beef, apples, and bread, it takes almost everything I have to ward off sleep long enough to set up my tent. There are only three tents and for obvious reasons, none of us trusts Zeke enough to offer him a place inside one of ours. I toss him a blanket and leave him to sleep by the fire.

I wish I could say I'm able to sleep peacefully, but before I know it I'm back in my nightmare. The smoke is choking me and clouding my vision. I'm running, always running, but from what, I still don't know. A voice cuts through the commotion, "We're here…" a female voice calls out from the distance. "It's almost too late…HURRY!" The last word, hurry, comes out as a loud forceful bellow and causes me to wake with a start.

Needing some air, I open the flap of my tent to let the fresh air wash over me. I walk outside and find Zeke huddled by what remains of the fire, the small flames shrinking into oblivion. He's not asleep, but instead is staring into the smoking ashes.

"What's the matter, you can't sleep either?" he says to me.

"I think I got about as much sleep as I ever do," I reply, not wanting to let him in on my dream.

"Doesn't seem like those other two share in our sleep deprivation problems," he says, motioning to the other two tents.

"Guess, not. I have to say I'm jealous. I could use some rest."

"How do you know them anyway?" Zeke asks.

"We're in training together," I answer, before I remember that I need to be more guarded in my conversations with Zeke. This may be a good opportunity for me to gain a little more insight into how the Eastern army operates, so I turn the questioning on him.

"So, what were you doing before you became an evil spy and ruined my life?" *Hmm, perhaps that didn't come out as subtly as I had intended.*

He winces at my words, like he's in pain, but it has no effect on me. Whatever regret he has for his actions can't make up for the fact that my little brother is off somewhere alone right now and probably being tortured.

"I didn't want this to happen, Arden."

"Yes you did. That's why you came to my school – to hunt me down. Remember?"

"I know, but I tried to stop it, I really did. This thing, this war – it's just so much bigger than you and me. It's impossible to stop."

"Is that so? Do you have a lot of experience with it? The war, I mean."

He puts his head in his hands and runs his fingers through his golden hair like he's trying to wipe away his memories. "Yes, I guess you could say I have some experience. The East does things a little differently than the West. We don't send our children away to shelter them for sixteen years. Instead, we're practically ripped from our mothers' wombs and thrown into battle. Our training starts pretty much as soon as we can walk. From the age of seven, they used me as a spy, or as a lookout, or had me running messages on the battlefield – however they could think to utilize me. The real fun began as soon as I was strong enough to hold a sword."

Full of bitterness, he spits his words out with disdain. It's hard not to pity him. I don't like seeing anyone suffer, even if they are my enemy.

"It seemed like it had been so long since I'd seen any real kindness, something truly unselfish. And then I saw you. You are so genuine, so raw. You haven't been corrupted by all of this ugliness. You have to believe me when I say the last thing that I wanted to do was hurt you or your family. You have a good heart, Arden."

"Yeah, I do don't I? And I bet you can't wait to get your hands on it," I reply harshly.

He looks up at me with sad eyes and says, "All I want to do is protect your heart, Arden, not rip it out."

I want to believe him. I want to think that someone from the East could have some decency. I want to, but I can't. I've seen what he's capable of and I know too much to be won over with some choice words.

Trion is the next to awake and he groggily stumbles out of his tent, letting out a big yawn. His red hair is even wilder and more un-coiffed than usual. He sees us and stops. "Oh… hi. I'm not interrupting anything am I?" he asks.

"Of course not," I say. "Don't be silly. I just couldn't sleep."

"OK, then," he says and takes a seat next to me. We take this time to get some food into our empty bellies – yet another meal of dried meat and apples. I'm beginning to hate apples.

Shortly after we begin eating, a very grumpy Kayla bursts out of her tent.

"What's going on out here? Could you *be* any louder? If I have to hear one more sob story about how the East creates killer babies, I think I'm gonna vomit."

My blood rushes to my cheeks causing me to blush.

"You didn't fall for that garbage did you, Arden?" she asks.

"Good morning to you too, Kayla. Please, come and have some breakfast with us," I say as nicely as I can manage.

We finish eating and pack up our camp, hiding the evidence of the fire before leaving. We mount our horses and resume our journey to Wellsport. As we ride, I watch the scenery change from dense forests to sweeping landscapes of tall grass and open fields. Eventually, we hit a rocky, unforgiving terrain and are forced to dismount our horses.

"We're getting closer," Zeke says. "We should reach the fortress tomorrow."

"You didn't say anything about a fortress," I say. "How are we supposed to get in and out of a fortress?"

"Just leave that to me," he replies.

"Oh sure, that sounds perfectly reasonable," Kayla says sarcastically.

The grey stony land that surrounds us has a cold callous quality to it and puts us all on edge. We try to travel quietly, but it's impossible since the gravel beneath our feet makes a loud crunching noise with each step. From behind a nearby rock, I hear a low, guttural grumbling sound. Something knows we're here and is not happy about it.

"Don't move!" Zeke barks. "These boulders are infested with stone dwellers. They aren't exactly hospitable to trespassers."

We all stop, fearful to take another step. A dark brown wrinkly hand appears from behind the rock, clasping the top of the rock with its long, yellow, claw-like nails. There's a horrible screeching noise, like nails on a chalkboard, as one of the claws pulls on the stone and yanks its owner upwards. I cringe when the creature reveals a portion of its head – just enough so that it can get a clear look at us. What I see alarms me. Its head is dark brown, like its hand, but it has brightly colored rings circling its face. Its eyes are black and unfeeling, like bottomless pits. I can't see its mouth, but the disturbing grumbling continues.

Within seconds, I notice hundreds of tiny black eyes popping out from behind the rocks, peering at us curiously from behind their stony safeguards, waiting for their cue.

"What are they doing?" Kayla whispers.

"Deciding whether or not to attack, I think," Zeke says.

"Why don't we just keep going?" Trion suggests. Then, he addresses the creatures, "We mean you no harm, we're just passing by and will be on our way now." He takes a step forward and is met with a golf ball-sized stone to the skull. He falls to the ground, blood trickling from the spot where the rock hit.

"Trion!" Kayla cries out, as she rushes over to his motionless body.

A rainfall of stones begins. Hundreds of rocks of all different sizes fill the sky, blocking out the sun's rays and creating a dark, solid cloud of destruction. I cower to the ground with my arms wrapped over my head, waiting for the first shots of pain to hit.

They never come. The sound of stones ricocheting off a hard surface fills the air and when I look upward I see that the stones are unable to reach us, blocked by an invisible force. Confused, I look to my companions. Trion is still unconscious from the blow to his head and Kayla is shielding him with her body, still waiting for the rocks to hit. When I locate Zeke, I'm taken aback to see that he's the one providing our protection. He's crouched on the ground, hands above his head, focused intently on the rocks above our heads. There's just the faintest hint of blue flowing from his body, creating a dome of protection. The stress on his face shows as he maintains the shield.

"Get…ready…to…run," he strains. He then begins whispering, his eyes rolling back in his head. Beams of blue light shoot through the shield in all directions and to my astonishment, the brown creatures begin running away in terror. I run to my horse, ready to make a break for it, but then I turn back and see that Zeke has collapsed and is lying still on the ground. I bolt over to him without thinking and scoop him up in my arms. He's still breathing, but his breath is shallow and his eyes remain rolled back. He feels frail in my arms, unlike the menacing threat I've been envisioning him as lately. I drag him to his horse and coerce Kayla to help me lay him over the back of it, positioned so that this head is dangling over one side and his feet the other.

Trion is still passed out and I offer to help Kayla place him on the back of her horse. She refuses and chooses to carry him herself, stating that Trion is scared of horses and she'll have no trouble lugging around his scrawny butt herself. I'm afraid that she'll slow us down by walking while her horse follows behind, but she's adamant. I tie Zeke's stallion to mine, and we head on our way.

We push forward on the path that we'd previously mapped out, keeping one eye on the rocks as we move ahead. As far as I can tell, the little brown creatures are not interested in bludgeoning us to death anymore, although I continue to feel as though we're being watched.

"So it looks like our friend here is a wizard," Kayla says. "You'd think he might've mentioned that before."

"Maybe he didn't see a need to mention it," I reply. "I mean, we didn't tell him what our skills are."

"True, but it still seems fishy to me," she says. "Anyway, aren't you supposed to be a Sensitive? Why couldn't you tell he was magic?"

Thinking back, it dawns on me that all of those times I felt electricity upon seeing Zeke must have been my reaction to his magic and not the chemistry I mistook it for.

"I think I may have felt it, but I just didn't recognize what it was," I explain.

"Well you sure seem like you feel *something*," she says.

"I'm only nice to him right now because he's helping us find my brother. That's all. I don't *feel* anything else," I say.

"Right… sure you don't. Just keep in mind that he's our enemy, alright?"

Looking at Zeke now, sprawled out across the back of a horse, and too weak to walk from the energy it took to save us, I must admit that I don't see him as my enemy. Not at the moment.

The sun is starting to slip beneath the horizon, so Kayla and I begin to set up camp, agreeing that we're not familiar enough with the landscape to make our way at night without Zeke's help. Kayla is about to lay Trion on the ground when he comes to and lets out a startled scream. The sudden noise takes Kayla off-guard and she winds up dropping Trion on the ground with a loud thud. He screams again as one hand goes to his back where he landed and the other to his swollen head.

"What were you doing?" he shouts at Kayla.

"I was helping you, you idiot!" she retorts.

I leave them to continue their bickering and go to help Zeke off the horse. He's still weak, but his eyes are back to normal and his breathing is restored. I help him slide off the horse and steady his feet on the ground. He's able to walk with my help. Having him so close to me like this sends bolts of electricity throughout my body. At least now I understand why.

"I heard what you said about only being nice to me because I'm helping you find your brother," he says quietly. "I want you to know that I don't blame you. I know I don't deserve your kindness."

"You heard that, huh?" I say, embarrassed at my words. "Listen, I know that you went through a lot back there to help us and I want to thank you. I owe you."

"No, you don't. You wouldn't even be here if it weren't for me. And trust me, Arden, there's much worse waiting for us up ahead."

"How much longer do we have? We have to be close by now, right?"

"Oh yes, we're close," he says as he raises his shaky hand, pointing in the distance. "In fact, we're practically there."

I follow the direction of his finger and in the distance I see a massive stone fortress sitting atop a hill, dominating the landscape. So that's where they're holding my little brother? Well, good for them. They're going to need a bigger fortress than that to keep me out.

CHAPTER 16

Welcoming

It's getting cold out, but none of us wants to light a fire for fear of attracting unnecessary attention to ourselves. Between the heavy blankets and our tents, we should be alright getting through the night. I can't bring myself to leave Zeke out in the cold in his weakened state after what he did for us, so I allow him to share my tent. Despite his condition, he is strikingly handsome, practically perfect, like he was made to taunt me. Still, he's an Easterner. He cannot be trusted.

And yet his actions are not those of an Easterner.

Maybe Kayla's right. My feelings for him could be more than just superficial attraction. Why would an Easterner help me rescue my brother? He must be risking a lot. An enemy would not do this. Maybe Zeke is not my enemy.

I'm so anxious to get to my brother that I have trouble falling asleep, so I wind up curled in a ball, listening to the wind whip against the tent and praying I don't hear any more grumblings from the rocks. Zeke passes out almost immediately, but I doubt he's getting much rest. He's tossing and turning and making a horrible groaning sound as if he's in pain. I want to go over to him and comfort him, but I don't. Admitting how I feel is one thing, but acting on it is another. I'm not quite ready to let Zeke know that I trust him.

Now that I have a moment to myself, there's one thing I can no longer ignore – my nightmare. It continues to follow me wherever I go, relentless in its quest for my attention. There must be a reason. After all, I am no ordinary person, I am a Sensitive. I didn't recognize the voice that was calling to me the other night and I'm not really sure what it was trying to tell me. Am I late for something? That last word sounded like a command. Someone wants me to hurry to them. But why? Does all of that destruction have something to do with the war?

I try to push the thought out of my head because it's scary and I'm not ready for that kind of fear. With these ideas struggling to overtake my mind, there's no way I'm getting any rest tonight.

Thoughts of Derek replace terrifying thoughts of war. I can handle Derek-related issues.

I have a clear definition of who Derek is to me, what he represents. Derek is my friend. Now he is my friend who kissed me. He crossed that line that has always been there, keeping us apart, making sure we stayed at a safe distance. Close, but never touching. I haven't thought of him that way before. I haven't let myself. We've never had that spark, that *electricity*. Perhaps I wasn't looking for it. His lips were so unexpectedly soft...

What will I feel when I see him again? Maybe my body will give me a sign like my knees going all wobbly or something. One can only hope.

Zeke is awake after only a few hours. He looks like he's gained a little bit of his strength back, but there are dark circles under his eyes and his face looks drawn and sallow.

"Trouble sleeping again?" he says to me with a smile.

"Me? Seems like you could use a visit from the Sandman yourself."

"I doubt either one of us is going get much rest from now on. We have some pretty terrible things ahead of us and we should be using this time to rest. We're going to need all of our strength and then some."

"Speaking of all of your strength, why didn't you tell me you could do magic?" I ask, trying not to sound like I'm interrogating him.

"Oh… I thought it was pretty obvious that you weren't dealing with any *normal* guy," he says with an exaggerated grin, which quickly disappears when he sees that I'm not at all amused. "Still not a good time for jokes? OK, then. I didn't tell you I was a wizard because I didn't want to alarm you. Do you really think Kayla would have agreed to go with me if she knew how powerful I am? I'm not a wizard like Trion is a wizard. He clearly doesn't know the kind of power he has yet. I've been at this a lot longer and I'm much more advanced. I'm capable of doing some pretty outrageous things."

"Now *that* I can believe," I say.

"Now, now, I thought we were being serious," he scolds.

"What did you do back there to those horrible little rock creatures? Why did they run away?"

"They ran because I induced fear in them – a fear so powerful that they believed their only option for survival was to flee from us and never return. I must say, I have a special knack for generating fear." The seriousness on his face and the tone of his voice make it clear that this time he's definitely not kidding.

"Whatever you did, I'm glad you were there to do it. It seems to me that we have a lot going for us with you in our corner," I say as I start making my move towards the front of the tent. "I think I've had just about enough of sitting around. Do you think the others are awake yet?" I ask.

"Maybe, maybe not, but I think you and I are on the same page – let's get out of here."

We leave the tent and the shock from the cold early morning air hitting my face jolts me to my senses. I'm wide awake. It's still dark out so I have to feel my way to the other tents, trying not to trip on a misplaced stone. I'm not sure whose tent I reach first or how I should wake up my victim, so I simply begin opening the tent flap. This is not one of my more brilliant ideas. I soon realize that the tent belongs to Trion. I know this because the sound of me opening his tent startles him awake and with a scream, he casts a light spell so bright that I'm completely blinded.

"Ahhhh!" he screams.

"Ahhhh!" I reply.

I'm still seeing spots when Kayla runs over from her tent, sword in hand.

"What is *wrong* with you two? Are you trying to get us killed?" she asks.

"I was just trying to wake you guys up," I explain sheepishly.

"Well congratulations. You've succeeded in not only waking us up, but anything within a 100 mile radius."

"I'm sorry alright," I say, still rubbing my eyes.

"As if my headache wasn't bad enough already," Trion complains.

"You're lucky all you have is a headache and a lump on the head. If you'd been hit with one of those giant rocks I'm not sure you'd still be here," Zeke says.

"Yeah, I feel really lucky right now," Trion replies.

The other three have to pack up our supplies since it takes a while before my vision readjusts to the lack of light. Eventually, the spots in front of my eyes disappear and we head off into the darkness. We leave the horses behind, hoping that we'll have a better chance of sneaking into the fortress on foot. It breaks my heart to let the horses go like that, without knowing where they'll go or if they'll survive. Kayla tries to help by tapping into her animal master skills and instructs them to go back to the fields we passed through on the way here. She thinks that they'll be happy there, and I agree. I hope the horses understand her and make it back safely. At least then we'll have freed someone on this journey.

As we walk, I start to hear new disturbances. I think the slithering sounds are what freak me out the most. The sound of scaly skin sliding slowly along the gravel near our feet makes my skin crawl. I can't see what's making the noise and because Zeke proposes that we refrain from using Trion's light spell, we continue to move forward blindly. We all agree that after the incident with the stone dwellers, we should listen to Zeke's recommendations.

The cold is starting to bother me. My movements are hindered by my aching, stiff joints and the forced clenching of my jaw to stop my chattering teeth has left me with a shooting pain in my head. It's difficult to focus. It can't be too long before the sun rises and drenches me in its warmth. We're nearly there too – the large fortress walls are within our reach now. Just a little while longer…

"We should discuss how we plan to get inside those walls," I suggest.

"Oh, I don't think there's going to be much to it," Zeke says. "The plan's pretty self-explanatory. Just follow my lead when we get there."

"If you say so," I reply. Kayla shoots me a look of disbelief.

By the time the sun finally shows its friendly face, we've already arrived at the stony walls and I find myself wishing that we were still protected by our blanket of darkness.

The fortress walls must be a hundred feet tall and are composed of dark grey stone with intermittent patches of moss. It looks like they were constructed ages ago. The monstrous walls are lined with about thirty guards set at even intervals on top of the walls' walkways. Each guard is armed with a sheath of arrows, and dressed head-to-toe in the standard Eastern purple and black. Being seen by these guards is the last thing that we want, so we make sure to stay close to the ground and hidden behind the rocks.

"What now?" Kayla whispers.

"Now we make our grand entrance," Zeke says before giving me a sideways glance. Stunning us all, he walks out from behind the rocks and begins yelling at the guards.

"What are you doing? Come back here! They'll shoot you!" I hiss.

He turns to me. "No, I don't think that they will," he says pointedly before turning back to address the guards. "Open the gates! We've arrived!"

Trion and I look at each other, both of us starting to panic. "What's he doing? He's going to get us killed!"

The big wooden gates blocking our entrance into the fortress slowly screech open to reveal an army of at least ten units of armed Eastern soldiers, each carrying different forms of weaponry to torment and inflict agony on their victims. Many have been given battle axes, some have crossbows, and the more vicious looking of them are carrying flails along with swords. The sea of purple and black begins to part, revealing a woman in a long purple velvet gown with a black satin train. I can't get a clear look at her face from this distance, but her hair is pale yellow and is done up in a fancy hairdo I would expect to see at prom.

The woman begins to move out of the fortress, shouting playfully, "Arden my dear! Come out come out wherever you are!"

Astounded, Kayla and Trion look to me for answers, but I don't know what to tell them. How does she know my name? I feel a dull pain in my gut and as the woman moves forward, her face becomes clearer. I can't believe my eyes. Or at least I don't want to. "Cici?" I whisper, still in shock. I collect myself as I realize what I've led us into. "It's a trap!" I scream. We get up to run in the other direction, but we're not fast enough. Before we can escape, a large net of blue light comes crashing down upon us, gathering us together like field mice.

I try breaking through the netting, but it's no use, the binds are strong and unforgiving. My body feels like it's on fire from the magic emanating off the rope and I scream out in pain. When I finally see who's providing this energy filled cage, my heart sinks. It's Zeke. I remain frozen in astonishment as I watch him concentrate on the netting, making sure his spell does not falter and we all remain neatly enclosed within his blue prison.

CHAPTER 17

Prisoners

"Well hello, brother, I wasn't expecting you so soon," Cici says to Zeke. "I thought she would at least put up a fight," she finishes, an evil smile forming on her perfectly red lips.

"You know how charming our family can be. But then again, it barely took any charm at all to deceive her. It turns out that this Westerner is a lot more gullible than we'd anticipated," he replies.

"I can see that. Well while you were away, the fun here was just getting started. I haven't yet had time to prepare everything for our Western friends' visit."

"Don't worry, sis; you always fuss too much anyway. I'm sure they'll find everything downright homey."

"Oh, you know me better than that. It's not the homey aspect I'm referring to," she says with a knowing look in her green, hate-filled eyes. "Where *are* my manners? Here I am standing with you and talking about our guests right in front of them. How rude of me!" She turns to address us directly, "Would you like to go

inside? You must be tired from your long journey and… truth be told, I simply cannot *wait* for you to see what surprises we have in store for you!" Her last sentence is clearly intended for me as she stares into my eyes.

With a flick of his finger, Zeke turns the blue netting into shackles around our wrists and ankles, connecting us all with a long blue chain. "Shall we?" he says politely as he leads us inside the gates. As we enter, the guards rip away our bags and all of our weapons, leaving us defenseless.

My mouth is so dry that my tongue is stuck to the roof of it. I have allowed Zeke to deliver my friends straight to the Eastern army. Three Westerners in a nice pretty package, tied with a neat little ribbon. I'm responsible for our capture. I can't look Kayla or Trion in the eyes. Have I led my friends to their deaths? They must hate me, and I don't blame them. Kayla has at least shown me some kindness by not pointing out the fact that she'd warned me about Zeke. She knew all along that he was just another Easterner. Why couldn't I see it too? I had sixteen years of preparation only to be fooled by some blonde hair and a set of pretty green eyes.

The Eastern soldiers snicker and spit at us as we walk by. One of them tosses a muddy boot at Kayla, leaving a dirty imprint on her back. Cici is quick to scold them. "That is no way to treat our guests!" she calls out, but I can tell that she's amused by it.

We enter the castle-like structure that must be the main part of the fortress. It's cold and damp, and smells of mildew and mud. I don't know where they're taking us, but Cici is in a hurry to get us there. With the chipper mood she's in, there must be something terrible waiting for us.

We travel through a great entryway filled with colorful hanging tapestries that depict various Eastern victories over the West, before taking an abrupt turn off to the side into a cramped hallway. The hallway leads us into a small, out of the way room that's empty except for an old writing table that holds a single quill, a bottle of ink, and some parchment. The walls of the room are covered in beautifully carved, dark wooden paneling, with each panel identically displaying a perfectly shaped lotus flower.

"Oh nice, this must be your yoga studio!" I say sarcastically, wanting them to know that they haven't broken me, that I'm not afraid of them.

"Shut up you twit! The lotus flower represents many things, but here it stands for survival and rebirth. It's one of many shapes that house great power, which you would know if you weren't such a Western fool!" Cici shouts.

She walks over to the writing table and dips the quill in the ink. She then begins drawing circular, scrolling patterns on a piece of parchment and when she's finished she's created a rather lovely picture. *I'm sure that's one to hang on the fridge*, I think, but decide to keep this comment to myself.

She holds up the picture and begins speaking a language that I haven't heard before. It sounds a little like "meedag tslyk cheekton" or what I translate to "my dog tastes like chicken." Hey, who am I to judge the East's secret passwords? The picture starts to glow a brilliant blue and the parchment rises from her hands. The glowing parchment floats over to one of the panels and upon touching its surface, the parchment bursts into flames, leaving a temporary imprint of Cici's design in blue smoldering embers on the wood and a few leftover ashes floating carelessly in the air.

The panel where the parchment touched begins shifting to one side. Next thing I know, an entire wall of wooden paneling opens, revealing a winding staircase leading downward into darkness.

"Right this way, dearies," Cici says and ushers us forward.

Trion gives me a worried look right before we begin our descent into the black – the blue light from our shackles lights the way.

As if the trip down the tiny winding staircase isn't bad enough, Cici begins humming a playful melody, adding insult to our situation. This girl has some serious issues.

A flicker of light from the depths below signals that we're nearing the end. It grows larger and brighter as we come closer to the bottom until we're standing directly in front of it and I see that it's just a torch on the wall, strategically positioned to welcome its guests.

We walk past the torch into an enormous circular stone room lit up with the glow of the many other torches placed around its perimeter. The first thing I notice about the room is that there's no floor in the center of it, only a deep, seemingly bottomless pit. The second thing I notice is that there are prison cells lining the walls, most of them are empty, but one of them is not.

"Arden!" he screams as he slams his body against the bars holding him captive.

"Pax!" I yell in agony. "Pax, I'm here now, I'll get you out! I promise!" Maybe this is a hasty promise to make, but I know that I won't rest until he's safe.

"Arden, look!" Pax shouts and points to the center of the room.

I look to see what he's pointing at, but the vision before me is so disturbing that it doesn't register. A bloody, mutilated figure dangles from the ceiling, suspended by chains. It's a young man. I can tell that he's alive because his struggle to breathe is causing exaggerated up and down movements in his chest. His head hangs down in front of his body, blocking his face from my view. He groans and lifts his head ever so slightly, as if it's the most difficult thing he's ever had to do.

No! *NO!* I think. No, this is *not* happening! Not to him. It can't be! His face is barely recognizable, but I know immediately.

The young man hanging before me is Derek.

CHAPTER 18

Bargains

The blood from Derek's body falls in tiny droplets into the black abyss below.

"What have you done?" I scream, falling to my knees, one hand finding my talisman and gripping it ferociously, while the other lands on top of my head, my fingers practically ripping out my own hair. It feels like I've just been punched in the chest – all of the air has been knocked out of my lungs and I'm left crumpled on the ground, staring up at Derek's broken form. I can't take my eyes off of him. A wave of pain washes over me, like I'm the one hanging from the ceiling. I cry out again, "No! Why him? WHY?"

Derek's not able to hold his wounded head up for more than an instant when he hears my screams. In a sick way this eases my pain since I can't bear to look him in his swollen eyes, which are now so engorged with blood that I'm not sure if he can even see at all. He lets his head drop back down and releases a small, barely audible groan from somewhere deep in his throat. This makes me think he recognizes my voice and knows that I'm here. A thought that I'm sure brings him no comfort.

My fighting instincts kick in and I scan the room, looking for some way to get us out. I'm the one who got us into this situation and I'll not let us die here at the hands of these animals. I think back to my time in the training camp and realize that we only succeeded when we decided to play by our own rules. If I apply the same logic here, then playing by their rules means that we all die.

I take a flying leap towards Zeke, whipping my blue chains over his head and wrapping them around his pale throat. I apply all the rage I've built up from Zeke's betrayal into choking the life out of him with his own stupid magic. I pull so hard on the chains that my knuckles turn white from the strain and the electricity from the magic singes the tiny hairs on my arms. He grasps at the chains, but I don't let up. Either he's dying or we're all getting out of here in one piece.

"Get off of him you Western dog!" Cici shouts.

While she's running towards me to pull me off Zeke, Kayla and Trion do as I'd hoped and use their chains to trip Cici and send her crashing to the ground. Kayla's on top of her in an instant. She pins Cici to the ground, viciously pushing her head close to the open pit. The six guards that accompanied us down here surround us, but seem too stunned to know what to do.

"You can't leave here without us," Cici wheezes as she tries futilely to fight Kayla off. "You'll die before you reach the top of the stairs."

I hate to admit it, but she's right. I didn't think this through. We can't take out all of the guards and Cici and Zeke without any weapons. Thanks to our surprise attack; however, we're the ones with the power at the moment. I decide to use our newfound leverage.

"Yeah, well I don't see why we would need both of you. Get Derek down now or I swear Zeke will die!" And then I use my last bit of strength to get my point across. Zeke, although much bigger than me, falls to his knees still clasping at the chains I've secured around his neck. It occurs to me at this moment that I'm using his own magic against him, which probably means that he could make the chains disappear with a flick of his wrist. I'm hoping that the shock from my attack has clouded his mind and he won't figure it out before Derek's released.

"Listen to her, Cici," Zeke screeches.

Cici commands the guards to let Derek down and none of us budges until he's been brought safely to the ground. The moistness on my hands makes the chain start to slip. I realize that I'm pulling so hard that I've cut into my own hands and I'm bleeding. Knowing that we don't stand a chance of escaping like this, I let the chain fall. Zeke collapses to the ground gasping for air and clutching his bruised throat. The black and blue marks are already starting to form on his flawlessly snowy white skin. I feel a gruesome kind of pleasure seeing the damage I've done. Kayla releases Cici and backs away from the pit.

"Why are you standing around? Get them!" Cici yells. The guards seem to regain their senses and one of them grabs me by the neck with his rough hand. He uses his other hand to point a dagger into my back and usher me into one of the prison stalls. Right now I don't care what they might do to me. At least Derek is down from that horrible contraption.

I hear Cici angrily murmuring to Zeke, interrogating him as to why he didn't release his spell and free the two of them from his magical binds. I guess he frightens easier than I thought.

My punishment comes in the form of a maimed, bloodstained body – Derek's body. The rest of the group is put into separate prison cells, but Cici has the guards toss Derek in with me. I feel shattered. His face is so mangled that I can hardly tell it's him. His nose is broken and his eyes are grotesquely swollen. His body hasn't fared much better. There are giant gashes all over his back, arms, and legs. They must have whipped him while he was hanging from the chains. The stress of the chains has left black bruises where they supported his weight. He's lost a lot of blood. Even through the red stains I can see that he's much paler than usual. He won't last long in this condition.

"Why did you do this to him?" I cry out. "He has nothing to do with this!"

"True," Cici replies, "but he was in the wrong place at the wrong time, so we decided to take him along for a little extra fun. I mean, who knew you two were neighbors?" she exclaims in her high-pitched voice.

The idea that they did this to Derek – a completely innocent person who doesn't even know anything about this realm or the war – is so revolting that I physically gag and have to swallow the bile creeping up my throat.

Derek tries to speak my name, AJ, but it comes out as a liquid gurgle from his busted lips.

"Shh, don't try to talk. Just lie still," I plead. I try to brush his face with my hand the way he did to me when I was injured. Either I'm too clumsy or his wounds are too fresh and deep because even the slightest touch from the back of my palm makes him wince.

"Fix him! Fix him NOW!" I demand. "If you want anything from us, you'll have to make him right again!"

"Or, we could just kill him. You're not really in a place to make demands," Cici corrects.

"You want to know about the Bravura training camp, right? Well that means that you need us. And if he dies, none of us are talking." I'm sure my friends won't be talking anyway, so I figure that this is a solid enough threat.

"You're a good little bargainer aren't you?" she says. "Very well, I'll send for a healer and we'll see what we can do." She sends Zeke to retrieve the healer, which disturbs me since I now know I can't trust him.

It feels like hours pass as we sit there waiting for the healer to arrive. I look around and see that the moisture in the air has caused black mold to spread across the prison walls, as if the evil in the place is a contagion. Derek continues to moan in my arms, his body cold and weak. From where they have me captive I can see directly into Pax's cell, which I'm sure is no accident. They want me to see that they have my little brother. They want me to know that they own me, and that I'm just a pawn in their sick game. All I can do is sit here staring into his big brown eyes. He looks more like a frightened boy of twelve now than the strapping young warrior I saw him as before. *"What did they do to you? Did they hurt you?"* I think as I look at him. To my astonishment, I hear his voice in return. It sounds distorted, like he's calling to me from far away, *"No, I'm fine. They were waiting for you."*

Have I totally lost it or did I really just hear that? And then it comes again, the distant warbled voice, *"We have to get out of here, they're insane. They'll kill us all."*

Whether real or not, I decide it's best not to ignore voices in my head. *"I'll think of something, I promise."* Again, with my promises.

"You know, while we're waiting, we could always see what these other two have to say," Cici suggests, her goal to scare us into submission. "What do you think? This one, the one who tripped me, looks like she can be pretty talkative. Guards! Get her out!"

Two colossal guards stomp over to Kayla's cell, smiling and snorting over the good time they're about to have. They unlock Kayla's cell and she charges them, almost knocking one over the ledge. They're too strong for her and in no time, they have her strapped to a wall. Her arms and legs are spread wide, leaving her vulnerable and in plain sight for all of us prisoners to witness her torment.

Cici approaches Kayla, "The Hanger, as we like to refer to it, is not our only form of punishment. You see, we have other, less traditional ways as well. My brother and I share a special talent for this sort of thing. Although – and I hope you don't think it immodest of me to say so – I've been blessed with a bit more power than him," she pauses, studying Kayla's face. "Most people break after only a short while. Let's see how long you last."

Cici has her back to me, facing a defiant Kayla. I don't know what she's doing, but without warning, my whole body is overtaken with vibration. It's only a matter of seconds before Kayla's look of determination fades and is replaced with outright fear. Based on what Zeke was able to do to a whole town of stone dwellers, I shudder to think what a concentrated dose of that stuff must be doing to Kayla. Cici continues with her mental torture while we all stand by helpless.

Magnified by the vibrations off the walls, Kayla's screams cut through the dank air as she thrashes against her binds, knocking the back of her head against the wall.

"Do you have anything you want to share with the rest of the group?" Cici goads.

"No!" Kayla growls like a rabid animal, frothy spit flying from her mouth.

"Are you so sure?"

And then suddenly the violent screams stop. Kayla's body goes stiff, her back arched in a distorted U shape, her face frozen in a look of terror.

"How about now, sweetie?" Cici toys.

Cici's torture fest is interrupted by Zeke and a very old man, who I assume must be the healer.

"Cici, what's this? I thought we were playing nice today," Zeke chides.

"Alright, she isn't talking anyway and I'm getting bored with her. Guards! Take this Western animal back to her cell."

Kayla's body goes soft and the two burly guards drag her limp form back to her cell. All I can think about is how I hope someday Kayla will be able to forgive me for this.

The hunched old man, wrinkled and grey, hobbles over to my cell. The cloudiness in his eyes tell me that he's blind, so I'm surprised when he says, "Oh my, this will take some time, yes indeed, he's badly injured."

"How can you see that? Aren't you blind?" I blurt out.

"You don't need eyes to tell that, I could smell the blood from the top of the steps."

The crumpled man stoops down, his joints making a horrid tearing sound as he bends his aged knees. The healer takes his pruned hands and places them softly on Derek's mangled body, causing him to moan. We sit in silence. A silence so loud that it's driving me crazy. I'm about to call out the old man for being a fraud when he pulls some herbs from a small leather pouch dangling at his side. He places the herbs in his mouth and gnaws at them with his dull teeth until I can see his saliva spilling out like mucky pond scum. He spews the wet mixture into a big gob in his upturned palm and then begins filling Derek's wounds with the stuff. He continues this process until Derek bears a striking resemblance to a swamp creature. Next, he pulls a vile of clear liquid from another pouch and forces it down Derek's throat. Derek chokes up some of the liquid and it comes out a cloudy pinkish hue, but he's able to keep most of it down.

"There now," says the old man. "With time, he should heal. He's fortunate that I got here before it was too late."

I can see the muscles in Derek's body relax and he's no longer groaning in pain. I'm grateful to the old man for bringing Derek comfort, but I can't bring myself to thank him.

"Perfect!" Cici exclaims. "Now that that messy business is over with, we can move on to more important matters." She has two of the guards hoist the old man up and hurry him out of the prison.

I know I'm grasping for straws at this point when I say, "I said I would help you when Derek is better. He isn't better yet, just look at him."

This comment sends Cici over the edge. "Do you want me to throw him down the pit right now and end this? Or better yet, how about we try our luck with your sweet little brother over there?"

Zeke meanders over. "Now, now, don't work yourself into a tizzy. She's technically right, and besides, what are a few more hours?" he says in a disinterested voice. He hovers by my cell an extra moment longer looking at me while I hold Derek. He looks…upset.

He then turns sharply on his heels, causing an abnormally large noise for such a small movement. Every little sound reverberates off the prison's stony interior and I can hear Kayla rocking back and forth in her cell, whimpering. I want to say something to Kayla to comfort her. I'm just about to when I hear the Pax-like voice in my head, *"Don't say anything, Arden! I know you, and I know you want to, but trust me, DON'T!"* When did my conscience get so reasonable?

I look over at Pax in his cell and wonder what will become of my once innocently naïve little brother – will he still be there when this is all over? He shakes his head at me as if reinforcing the imaginary Pax who has invaded my brain. I figure both Pax's can't be wrong, so I decide to listen to them and keep my mouth shut.

I should have known better than to stare at Pax.

Cici lets out a haughty sigh. "OK, I've had about enough. I'm not being bossed around by some Western idiot. She's *our* prisoner, remember?" she yells. "Guards! Grab the boy!"

"No!" I scream as loudly as I can, throwing myself against the bars, trying to shake myself free. Zeke whips around to look at me. His eyes are wide with terror.

"Wait!" Zeke shouts. "She'll tell us everything, I know it. There's no need for this!"

"What is *wrong* with you?" Cici yells at Zeke. "I know she'll talk because otherwise her sweet little brother is dead. Now, *move it* guards!"

Pax looks so frightened and panicked –like a caged animal waiting to be slaughtered. "Arden!" he shouts at me.

"Hold on Pax! It'll be OK!" I yell. Screaming at Cici, I say, "I'll tell you anything you want to know. Just don't hurt him."

"Oh, I'm afraid it's too late for that, honey. I'm changing up the rules of the game – we're going by the house rules now," Cici responds. "First, we'll hurt him, and then you'll talk. Then we'll hurt him again, and then you'll talk some more. Got it?"

"If you touch one hair on his head…"

"What? You'll cry?" she says laughing. "Besides, darling, I think you know that it's his heart we want, not his hair."

"What's she talking about, Arden? What about my heart?" Pax shouts.

"Oh, the poor dear is too young to even know why he's here. Honestly, I don't know why you Westerners shelter your young so!" Cici exclaims.

Pax scurries to the rear of his cell as the guards approach him. With his back to the wall, he cowers to the ground.

"Where do you think you're going? There's nowhere for you to run to boy," one of the guards taunts. They yank him by his arms and drag him out of the cell, his feet scraping against the stony floor while he kicks and shouts.

"You know where to put him boys," Cici says.

"Stop it! I'll kill you, I swear it!" I yell out.

"Oh please, you're wasting your breath," she replies.

"Cici, really, we can do this thing another way," Zeke interjects.

"You know, I'm really starting to question your loyalty, brother. One more word from you and I'll have the guards string you up as well," she replies.

I look over at Pax and see that the guards have chained him to the wall where Kayla had been. I can't let them hurt him. I just can't. Cici isn't planning on playing with Pax's mind. She's planning on killing him.

Zeke sneaks over to my cell and whispers, "Focus on the pain, Arden. Focus on the burning."

"What are you talking about?" I reply too loudly, my voice bouncing off the walls.

"Just do it! Think about what you want to happen and make it happen," he quietly commands.

It takes me a moment to realize what he means. I do feel a pain...a burning. In my chest – right where my heart is. *This is the only way I can help him. I have to try, even if it kills me.*

I focus on the burning, trying to block everything else out. The pain intensifies. It feels like my heart is swelling in my chest and I feel a snap like my ribs are cracking. I see blue light from all directions coming at me, disappearing into my body through my chest. Zeke collapses on the ground in front of my cell as I steal the aether from his body. Across the pit, Cici cries out and falls to the floor.

I feel powerful. Invincible. I look down at my hands and they're glowing blue. My entire body is surrounded by blue light.

"Now!" Zeke cries from the floor.

I regain my focus and think about Pax and escaping. I picture the chains on his body breaking – and they do. I picture Cici and the guards being thrown against the walls so hard that their heads bleed and they're knocked out – they are. The entire prison begins to quake as the energy contained in my body shakes its foundation. Bits and pieces of rock begin to fall from the walls, crashing to the ground. Then, I picture the bars of our prison cells busting open, and they fly off the hinges towards the pit in the center of the room.

What I don't picture happening is Zeke getting caught beneath the bars.

"Run!" is the last thing I hear him scream before the darkness of the pit consumes him.

CHAPTER 19

Viking Ninjas

I feel lightheaded like I'm about to pass out. I can barely stand and the deafening sounds of warning horns being blown throughout the fortress isn't helping me focus. *They must know what I've done. They must be coming to get me.* I take about two steps forward before I collapse.

Two large, burley arms catch me before I hit the ground. "Arden…what have you done," the owner of the arms says.

"Kenlin?" I croak.

"Yes, it's me. We're here to get you out."

I force my eyes open and I see that he's not alone. There are two other large men, dressed in animal skins, who are busy gathering the rest of my friends. With the swords they have strapped to their backs, these guys look like a cross between Vikings and ninja warriors.

"Arden, you must stay strong. You must keep moving. Ask no questions. Follow us now. We have only a little time," Kenlin instructs.

I do as he says and use whatever strength I have left to walk forward out of my cell. I concentrate on one step at a time. Pax runs over to me and puts my arm over his shoulder to help me walk.

"Arden," he says tearily. "I...I..."

"Not now," Kenlin interrupts as he scoops up Derek from the floor of the prison.

The other two men help Trion and Kayla out of their cells. Trion is weak, but looks alright. Kayla is scared at first to leave her cell, but after a little coaxing from Trion, she's able to move on her own. I think she understands what they want her to do, but I'm not certain she fully comprehends what's going on.

On our way out of the dungeon, next to the welcome torch, is a hook holding the bags that contain our guide books and coins. It seems too good to be true, but we don't have time to debate the issue and we can't leave them here, so we take them with us.

Even with Pax's help, I feel weak as we climb the twisting stairs out of the dungeon. Kenlin, as strong as he is, carries Derek without struggle. I feel a constant tingling throughout my body as if magic is near.

We arrive at the top of the staircase to find that the doorway out of the dungeon is wide open. We move as stealthily as possible out of the dungeon and through the small room. A shiver runs through me as the dark wooden panels slide shut behind us like they were waiting for us to leave.

Kenlin, along with one of the men he came with, takes the lead, while his other enormous friend follows behind the group. They move with grace and agility and know exactly where to go. We pass through the hallway and arrive at the great entryway to the castle. Kenlin motions us forward to the other side. We tiptoe our way across the stony floor, careful not to make any sound, but I'm not able to stay as quiet as the rest of the group. My version of tiptoeing is more of a soft thud.

Kenlin directs us into a servant's room. One of the men lifts open a hatch on the floor and orders us to go in. Kayla, still in shock from her torture, begins panicking and it takes both of Kenlin's companions to force her down. Trion tries to comfort her along the way. Once inside, we begin running down a long corridor.

"This passage will take us to the outside kitchen, located at the edge of the property. The Hebelcaan tribesmen are here attacking the front of the fortress to cause a distraction. We should be able to escape this way unseen," Kenlin explains.

Sure enough, when we reach the end of the underground corridor, we lift the hatch and find ourselves in a large overcrowded kitchen. A kitchen filled with scared servants, all hiding from the commotion taking place outside at the front of the fortress. None of them look to be fighters and I get the distinct impression that they just want us to get out of their kitchen as quickly as possible. We gladly oblige. Once outside the kitchen, I can see the smoke from the fiery weapons that the Eastern soldiers are flinging over the fortress walls. I hope the Hebelcaan came prepared.

We sneak away to the edge of the wall and find a rope hanging over the side.

"This is how we entered and this is how we're getting out of here," Kenlin says.

"I'll go first," one of the Viking ninjas says. He makes climbing the wall look effortless and is up at the top in a matter of moments. He waits, perched on top of the wall for the rest of us to join him.

We each take turns climbing up the wall and I'm able to pull myself over with some help. When everyone else is over, Kenlin takes the rope and ties it around Derek's body. Both of Kenlin's men are still on top of the wall and they help pull Derek up and gently lower him down the other side. They move slowly so that they don't needlessly knock his body against the stony wall, but it's inevitable that Derek's skin gets scraped up in the process. I can hear his moans from the other side.

Once everyone is over, Kenlin pulls out a curved horn and blows. The horn's upward sloping curvature results in a distinct melodic vibration that reminds me of a woman humming. Almost immediately, we see a fleet of horses rush away from the fortress walls as the main force pulls back and heads over the rocky terrain.

Kenlin has six sturdy horses waiting for us to complete our escape. Pax helps me heave myself onto one of them before helping Kenlin place Derek over the back of one of the other horses. Kenlin rides with Derek to hold him steady and Pax and the two other men each get their own horses. Trion helps Kayla onto a horse and she seems to settle in once she is on top of her steed. She begins talking to it gently, saying things like "good horsey, nice horsey."

We ride as fast as possible for the next few hours, following Kenlin as he steers us towards safety. Eventually, it's too dark to ride and we're forced to stop and make camp in a patch of woods we've entered. I'm relieved when we stop because I don't think I could hold myself up any longer. My body is weak and I need rest. If it weren't for my natural riding abilities, I don't think I would have made it this far. I'm worried about Derek and Kayla too. I'm sure they need to rest as much as I do.

Kenlin and the two men create a fire and promise to keep guard throughout the night while we sleep. Kenlin places Derek beside the fire. As soon as he's safely in his spot, I slide in next to him and slip off into oblivion.

CHAPTER 20

The Tattoo

The sun beating down on my face only intensifies my throbbing headache. It seems I was too tired to dream last night, so I got more rest than usual. I still find myself wishing that Trion would use his light spell to suck the light out of the sun so I can get more. I make myself open my eyes and use my tired arms to push up into a seated position. My movements are slow and deliberate. I feel a dull aching all over my body. Even my toes hurt. It especially hurts to breathe. Maybe I really did crack a rib – it certainly feels that way.

I look around and see that Kenlin and the Viking ninjas are standing guard a little ways off and the rest of the group is still asleep.

Derek's lying next to me on his back. His wounds have drastically healed; the red inflamed gashes are now mostly closed and have changed from an intense fiery red to a subdued pink. Seeing him this way, I can feel my heart splitting, tearing apart inside of me and leaving me with shredded pieces of what was once a complete person. I gaze down at his bruised face – *is that one of those patented Derek smiles?*

"So this is what it takes to get you to notice me, huh?" he croaks, his dry throat altering his voice.

"You're seriously trying to make jokes right now?" I softly chuckle, as my eyes threaten to tear up at Derek's resolve to see the silver lining in even the cruelest situations. "Don't talk. You need to rest."

"What better time is there? I finally have your complete attention."

"OK," I say softly, "What do you wanna talk about?"

"Well, for starters, were you surprised when I kissed you?"

"You were just taken prisoner in another realm and *that's* what you want to know?"

"Hey, I've got my priorities," he says, laughing a little.

My face flushes. I know what he wants me to say. He wants me to confirm my feelings for him. After our kiss I ran like the coward that I am, too scared to face this type of emotion. I convinced myself that I had far too many other things to deal with. Now, after finding him on the verge of death, it seems like this is the only thing that actually does matter. I bend down and kiss him on his damaged lips.

He doesn't wince. There's no pulling back. He reaches up and draws me closer like he's trying to meld our lips permanently together. There are no questions in my mind now. The threat of Derek being wiped away from this world, of no longer existing, was all I needed to see the truth. It's always been right in front of me. There's no way around it. We belong to each other.

The rush from our kissing makes my head throb more and I have to stop to catch my breath. I instinctively put my hand on my chest over my talisman. Derek reaches up and moves my hand and talisman aside.

"What's this?"

"What?" I ask.

"This mark on your chest. When did you get a tattoo?"

"Um, I didn't." I look down to see what he's talking about and there's a little green mark over the spot where my heart's located. It looks like a little leaf. "Oh wow. I wonder if tapping into my heart did that," I say before I can stop myself.

"What are you talking about, AJ? Are you OK?" Derek asks. "I know you're not emotional, but I don't think using your heart gives you tattoos."

"No, it's not that. I just have a… different kind of heart, I guess you could say. I'll explain it to you later."

"I already knew you had a special heart," he says placing his hand over the leaf. "You know, AJ," he says as he looks at me, "it's always been you. Ever since the day I met you. You're the one."

I feel my heart skip, causing me a little pain, but I do my best to refrain from flinching. Kenlin sees us and comes over, taking a seat next to me.

"That was a risky thing you did back there, Arden," he says, purposely interrupting our moment. I don't think he can help but act the part of a protective father. He's so used to it by now.

"Using your gift like that can kill you," he continues. "Each time you do it, you'll be brought closer to death. That mark you have there is left over from where the aether entered your body. Let it be a reminder that your gift comes with a price."

"I know, Kenlin, but what was I supposed to do? I had to get us out of there. I didn't know you were coming," I explain. "By the way, how did you know where to find us?"

"I tracked you here. After Cici took Pax and Derek, I knew who to look for. I'm just sorry I wasn't able to stop her in the first place. I've let you down as a guardian," he says.

"Please don't say that," I say. "You saved us. We're alive because of you."

"Thank you for that, Arden," he says. "And it's my intention to keep you all alive."

While we're sitting, Kenlin gives us some flat pita-like bread he has with him and we devour it greedily, getting bits of bread all over ourselves. "Marion would be quite disappointed if she could see what slobs you've turned into," he says.

"Where is Marion?" I ask.

"When Cici and a group of Easterners broke into our house that night to take Pax, Marion tried to save him by pulling him out of Cici's arms. Cici was too strong and used her fire magic to burn Marion," he explains.

"What? Is she OK?"

"Yes, I think so. Marion was burned badly on much of her arms and went home to this realm to seek treatment. I haven't seen her since. I came looking for you as soon as I got the chance. I'll send word to her home to let her know that we're OK."

Kenlin gets up from his seat and walks over to Pax. He taps him with the point of his boot. "Rise and shine sleeping beauty. There'll be no dilly-dallying today."

Pax grumpily sits up, rubbing his sleepy eyes. Trion is the next to awake and he gently rouses Kayla. Kenlin tosses them all some bread.

I try to cheer up grumpy Pax by mentioning a topic I think he'll find amusing – namely the fact that I'm now officially crazy and am hearing voices in my head.

"You're not hearing voices," Pax says. "Well you *are*, but not like how you think. I heard you talking to me from my cell and I answered you. It's part of being a Sensitive. You have some psychic ability and can communicate with peoples' minds. I wasn't surprised when I heard your voice in my head."

"How do you know that?" I ask shocked at the idea that my little brother is now teaching *me*.

"I asked Marion and Kenlin about it after you told me what you were. No big deal," he answers.

When did he get so smart? Then I look at him, I mean *really* look at him, and I see a change. He seems more…serious. Like he's lived a thousand lifetimes during his young life. I wish I could have protected him from all of this; preserved his youth just a little while longer. If only I hadn't been so blind.

"OK, my turn," Pax says. "How did you do that thing with my chains and the prison doors? And how did you knock everyone out all the way from your cell? You're not a wizard, right?"

I look over at Kenlin for reassurance that it's OK to tell Pax and he gives me a nod.

"Have you ever wondered why the Bravura are different?" I ask. "Why we were sent away?" Then I tell him about the fifth chamber and aether. I tell him about how the East uses us, the Bravura, against our own people. He takes the news surprisingly well – almost like he was expecting it. I'm amazed at his maturity.

Derek, however, definitely wasn't expecting any of this. His eyes are as wide as silver dollars. Even though he doesn't ask for it, I give him a complete run down. I explain who I really am and tell him about our different realms and the war. It feels good coming clean to Derek. He doesn't say anything while I'm speaking, but takes it all in. He looks at me and says, "Wow, AJ, I knew you were a complex girl, but you managed to bring the term *complicated* to a whole new level."

"Does this mean that you're sorry about what happened?" I ask, hoping he knows what I'm referring to and that he doesn't make me say it.

"How can I be sorry that you've finally let me in? It's what I've *always* wanted. I can't regret anything that brings me closer to you."

After everything he's been through he's still the one making me feel better when I know that I should be the one comforting him. I'm starting to feel guilty that I don't have better nurturing abilities.

"OK, enough. You guys are totally grossing me out," Pax complains, tossing a piece of bread at my head.

Trion is busy keeping Kayla calm, so I'm not sure how much of the conversation he heard. Kayla is staring at the horses we rode here on. I'm growing concerned about how long it'll take for her to get back to normal.

As I'm sitting here, there's one unresolved issue gnawing at my brain. I almost don't say it, but then the words come slipping out of my mouth. "Do you think that Zeke was actually helping us the whole time?" I say to the group.

That question alone is enough to snap Kayla back into reality for a split second. "Have you completely lost your mind?" she yells at me before muttering something that sounds a little like "my little pony..." Trion stares at me from his seat like he can't believe what I'm saying.

I ignore the fact that even Kayla, in her disturbed state of mind, can see that this thought is crazy, and continue, "He's the one who told me how to save us."

"We can't know for sure," Kenlin says. "But I did find it odd that the doors to the dungeon were wide open when I arrived."

"I'm sorry, Arden, but I have a hard time believing that Zeke was anything other than a backstabbing Easterner after what he did to us. He betrayed our trust and locked us in a dungeon, don't forget," Trion says.

Was. Trion said Zeke *was,* implying that he no longer *is.* I can't shake the feeling that Zeke's intention was to help us all along, and now we refer to him in the past tense because he's gone. Because he helped *me.*

I see Derek studying my face and I know that he's trying to read my reaction. Thankfully, I have a pretty good poker face. I don't want to give him any reason to doubt my feelings now. Besides, I've never had to question whether or not Derek was trying to kill me.

After a while, Trion walks over to me, his face displaying his lack of sleep. Rubbing the crust from his eyes, he stoops beside me. "Look, Arden, Kayla isn't doing well. She was talking to herself all night and I think she was crying in her sleep. I'm really worried about her."

"I know Trion; I'm worried too. I think you need to take her back to the training camp so that she can be cared for there. Marcus will know what to do."

"That's what I was thinking too, but…"

I can see the concern in his eyes. He's worried about me, wondering how I'm going to get through this journey without the

rest of them. Because he feels a responsibility to keep me safe. And because he just plain cares.

"Don't worry about me, Trion; I've got this covered. Plus, I have protection here," I say motioning to Kenlin and the Viking ninjas. "I mean, look at these guys."

He looks relieved, taking my hands in his, "OK, but try to stay safe, will you?"

"I will. Seriously, now go."

He goes back to his spot near Kayla and tries to focus her attention by gently turning her face towards his. She seems confused, like she doesn't remember where she is, and he has to calm her down by making her focus on his eyes. I hear him tell her it's going to be OK. He takes both of the gold coins from their bags. Trion holds one in his hand and places the other in hers. He directs her to repeat his words. They continue staring into each other's eyes as they recite The Call of the Bravura and disappear from sight, leaving a giant hole in my chest.

CHAPTER 21

Balance

After Trion and Kayla leave, no one is feeling very talkative. We sit quietly, all of us worried about Kayla and wondering if she'll get back to normal.

Eventually, I break the silence. "Kenlin, have you heard any news about our family – about where our parents and Dannia are right now?"

"No, I haven't heard anything, but I have an idea where they might be," he replies. "I'll begin a search for them tomorrow. For now, we have to focus on getting Derek back to his realm."

"What do you mean?"

"As you know, Arden, our realm can't support the presence of outside forces – objects or people. We must maintain the balance of aether. Derek remaining here puts our entire world in jeopardy and risks his life in the process. In his weakened state, he won't last long. We need to bring him back home."

"So, I'll just use my coin and we'll go back now. He'll be fine then, right?"

"It's not that easy," Kenlin replies. "The coin doesn't contain enough magic to bring all of us back. We need to get to a node, or a focal point of aether, where magic is at its strongest. The closest one is Mt. Gracon. With the added strength of the aether at Mt. Gracon, you'll be able to use your Bravura coin to return Derek to his home, where he belongs."

I feel a sick pang in my stomach as he finishes his sentence. Like I'm going to puke. In the past, I would've thought it was just a reaction to the bad news. Now I know better. My feelings mean more, especially this particular feeling. I look around the campsite in search of the cause. It doesn't take long to find it. Coming closer to us, its pace quickening as my stomach turns, is a dense white cloud situated close to the ground. It pours over the green forest covering until it's only a few feet away.

"Everyone on your horses, now!" I yell.

Everyone jumps to their feet. The fog begins swirling together, twisting and turning until a beastly form emerges, resembling a wolf. It turns its red eyes towards me.

"They're here!' Kenlin shouts. "Head to Mt. Gracon! Quickly!"

Without hesitation, we mount our horses. Derek's still too weak to ride on his own, so we share a horse. I make sure to hold onto him tightly so that he doesn't fall.

Our horses are more than fast. They're large, white steeds that move at a blinding pace. Even with how fast we are the creature is not deterred. It continues to chase us with little effort, keeping a distance of a few hundred yards behind us. The fog maintains its beastly shape, splitting its body in two only now and then to get around a tree or a rock. The creature doesn't want to catch us – it would have no problem doing so if it did. Its purpose is to watch. I feel my hands start shaking when I think about who could be controlling it.

We cover a vast amount of ground in a short time. I know when we're close to Mt. Gracon because I can feel the aether in the air. It's like the earth is pulsating with magic, alive with an energy that I didn't know existed. I can't even imagine what it would feel like to have this type of energy stored inside of me. I can see how it would be too much for a body to take.

Interspersed between flashes of panic shooting through my brain, I keep reminding myself that I'm bringing Derek to safety. That he needs me to do this. I have to be strong for him.

"Look! On the horizon!" Kenlin yells from his horse.

Looking through the trees, I see that this is no ordinary place. Even from a distance, the hill of bones is impressively unnerving.

CHAPTER 22

The Calling

Following Kenlin's lead, we steer our horses towards the outline of an enormous skeletal man, half-encased by the earth and half-protruding bone, as if he's trying to force his way from the ground that's holding him captive. The gigantic man must have died some time ago. Judging by his huge, claw-like fingers grasping at the air, he didn't go willingly. I can't imagine what was able to take down a person of this size. He's at least 500 feet tall. Even more unsettling is that there's a passageway running right over his skeleton. The road starts at his tailbone, slopes upward about 50 feet over his ribs, and continues back down his neck, through his mouth, and into his skull.

As we get closer to the skeleton, the horses become agitated. They rear and I can barely hold Derek in place. Kenlin leads us to a spot near the giant's foot that's protected by a cluster of evergreens and tells us to dismount. Our horses run off in the other direction.

"See there?" he says, pointing to the giant skull. "That's where we need to go. The aether is strongest at that point. Now run!"

I move to grab Derek, but freeze when I see what's next to me. The creature is standing right beside me, twitching its cloudy head from side to side as it looks me over.

A familiar voice cuts through the trees.

"Oh, Arden, you didn't think it would be that easy did you, dear? I've got to give you credit, you certainly have a lot of heart." The high-pitched sound of her voice hurts my ears.

"Cici?" I cry out in disbelief as she emerges from out of the forest, flanked by several armed men. The cloud creature prances over to her and sits on its haunches at her side, leaving little puffs of cloud in its wake.

"You're going to die now," she says.

The armed men spread out behind her and she raises her hands in front of her. A glowing blue sphere of light forms in between them. She pulls her hands inwards towards her chest and then pushes them forward forcefully, releasing a ball of blue fire at me. I roll on the ground to avoid the flames.

Pax pulls me up and leads the sprint towards the skeleton. Kenlin and the Viking ninjas release a rain of arrows on Cici and her men, giving us enough time to get a head start. We scramble up the hill with restored energy. As we pass over the giant's ribs, I hear a peculiar noise inside my head, like a distant echo of many voices, all jumbled together. My stride slows to a stop as I see what's before me. In the distance beyond the skull, linked by chains, are rows upon rows of people on the verge of death. Their frail legs are barely able to hold their pale, skeletal bodies up as they stand, chests puffed out, heads back, swaying subtly as if they could fall at any moment. There are thin blue streams of light coming from the sky and entering into their chests, where their hearts are located. Their bodies are giving off a thick, black smoke that has found its way up the hill, clouding our vision. It smells like burning flesh. I know immediately that these must be Bravura. At the end of each row of Bravura is a clear sphere that looks like a giant snow globe, with blue light swirling inside. I stare ahead in disbelief and before I know it, my feet are taking me away from Pax and Derek and towards the Bravura.

"What are you doing?" Derek shouts.

"Stay with Pax! I'll be back!" I respond and keep running towards the Bravura.

Another ball of fire flies past me, missing me by inches. Cici is out for my blood. I'm glad because that means that Pax and Derek only have her Eastern soldiers to deal with. Kenlin and his men can handle them.

The smoke from the bodies gets thicker as I approach, causing my eyes and lungs to burn. It's difficult to see and I gasp when my hand brushes against one of the bodies. I didn't realize how close I was. The voices in my head are so loud now. The sound is piercing – so many jumbled voices shouting at me. I feel like screaming. Then, one voice rises above the others, quieting the rest.

"This way," it says.

"I'm coming," I find myself responding. I recognize the voice. I've heard it before. My feet carry me towards the sound. My eyes

are so watery that I can barely see where I'm going. It doesn't matter. I don't need to see. I know where to go.

I reach a spot in the middle of a row. I stop and turn.

"You came for us," a girl's voice says.

I look at the body where the voice is coming from. Through my blurry vision, I can tell it is a young girl, maybe my age. She's rail thin; her ribs are sticking out of her chest through her thin linen shirt. I now see where the smoke is coming from. The blue light entering her body has left a large black mark that covers her entire chest – not a cute little leaf like the mark over my heart. This black cancer is continuously giving off a thick cloud of smoke as it eats away at her. This is what happens when you take in too much aether.

Her mouth is not moving. Her eyes are not focused. Yet, I know that she's the one speaking to me.

"My name is Elda. I've been calling to you. I was hoping that you'd hear me."

"Me? Why me?"

"Because you're one of us. Because you have the power to free us."

"But I don't know what to do! I don't know how to get you out!"

"You must save us. No one knows we're here, except for you. You must tell the Western Kingdoms."

I look around at the chained Bravura and begin to understand. These could be my friends. Kayla and Trion could be here. One day Pax could be chained-up like this. These are my people and they need me to help them.

I try to collect myself. In the nose, out of the mouth. Think. "I didn't see any guards. The East wouldn't have left you unprotected. Who's watching you?"

"The guards were called away, but the wizard is still here."

"Yoohoo! Arden! Where have you run off to?"

I look up and see a flash of light a few rows away from me. Cici is searching for me. I have to act fast. I take the only hard object I have, my talisman, and remove it from my neck. I raise it high in the air, preparing to bring it smashing into Elda's chains. My talisman is on fire in my hand, but I don't care. I begin hacking away at the chains. To my surprise, they begin to break. My talisman is much stronger than I'd thought. I look down at my hand and it's glowing. The silver medallion is furiously bubbling; its middle turned to liquid, yet it maintains its circular shape. The blue light is no longer entering Elda's body; it's being redirected into my talisman. Now free from the aether, Elda is lying on the ground, curled in the fetal position. I feel a rush of joy when I see her chains breaking. I may be able to save her after all.

In an instant, I'm aware that my surroundings have changed. The smoke around me has parted. I hear a growl and turn to see Cici's wolf by my side staring at me. On my other side I hear a bellowing voice as if through a loudspeaker, "You dare to disrupt my harvest?"

I whip my head around and see a man floating towards me. His feet hover about a foot off the ground. The black robes that he wears flutter behind him in contrast to his long white hair. His voice is deep and angry. His eyes are filled with hate. I feel a hand grab me by the throat and lift me off the ground away from the chains, but there's no one near me. The invisible hand rotates me slowly in the air until I'm facing the floating man, still several feet away.

"Now you're mine!" Cici's voice comes at me from behind. She screams in rage and I feel heat rushing towards me. The hand releases me and I drop to the ground as a fire ball rushes past me towards the man in the black robes. It would have hit him square in the chest, but he places his hands in front of him and blocks the fire before it has a chance to strike.

"You fool!" he yells.

"I didn't...uh..." Cici responds.

I look at my talisman and at Elda. The aether that was meant for her is still taking hold of the medallion in my hand. I look up from the ground at the other Bravura and hold my talisman high, not really knowing what to do. Another beam of light is sucked away from the Bravura closest to me, entering my talisman. I'm jolted back from the force. The Bravura falls to the ground. It takes both of my hands to point the talisman at the man in the black robes, but as soon as I do, I release a force so strong that it causes a massive explosion. I'm thrown backwards several feet. My ears are ringing and the smoke is so thick now that I can't see.

I shakily get to my feet and yell, "I'll come back for you," before running in what I hope is the direction away from the man in black and Cici.

I have to get Pax and Derek out of here.

Just as I find my way out of the maze of Bravura, I feel a jarring that causes me to turn back. The smoke has lessened and I can see that a blue dome surrounds the Bravura. The wizard must be focused on protecting his crop.

I run to the giant skeleton and see that Kenlin and his men are still fending off the Eastern soldiers from the top of the hill. I'm coming from the other direction, so I think I have a clear shot around to the mouth of the skeleton.

I know exactly where to go because I've been here before. Or at least my subconscious has. This all feels familiar to me because Elda has been sending me visions of this moment. I see now that what I thought was a hill in my dream has turned out to be the sternum of the giant. Derek and Pax are waiting for me there while Kenlin and his men continue to fight. I hear a sharp, high-pitched scream from behind me. Fire flies past me. Pax and Derek see me and start running down towards the direction of the skull.

As we approach the skull, I can feel the aether collecting in that one, concentrated area. I clutch at my bag tightly as a fireball whizzes past my head, scorching the end of my hair. Then it happens.

I trip on part of a bone sticking out of the ground and I tumble forward, bouncing off parts of bones and dirt where the giant's neck

should be. All the while, I hold onto my bag as tightly as possible. I can't lose my coin. Not now.

Pax and Derek have to fall to the ground to avoid the flames flying at us and they end up sliding down to the neck on their backs until they reach me. Scraped and bruised, we don't have time to think. We yank ourselves off the ground and run until we burst through the mouth of the skull.

I see a ball of fire hurtling towards Pax, seconds from making him a new addition to this gravesite. Coin in hand, I snatch Derek and Pax by their wrists. "Take me home, take me home…" I plead just as the fire makes impact.

I can hear his screams ringing in my ears as we're wrenched away.

CHAPTER 23

Obligations

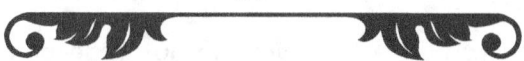

We land sprawled on the earth near the base of the old oak tree, like the giant just spewed us from his enormous mouth. Pax is still screaming, though the sound is partially muffled by his face lying in the dirt. His back is red and blistered and the remains of his shirt are melted to his marred skin.

"Pax! Pax!" I yell. "Pax are you OK?"

He responds with more screams.

From deep in the woods, I see a figure emerge – it's Marion.

"Who's hurt? Pax, is that you?" She sees him and gasps, placing her hands over her mouth. Her hands and arms are wrapped in clean, white bandages.

"Marion! What can we do?" I shout.

"Stay put! I'll be right back!" she commands before running back towards our house.

I feel so helpless just sitting here next to Pax, whose agonizing wails continue to flood the forest. He's in so much pain that I don't think he can comprehend anything I say to him.

Derek is hunched over near the tree, not saying a word. The travel must have been too much for his body to handle.

My entire world is crumbling down around me and all I can do is stand here and watch it happen.

"Marion! Hurry, PLEASE!" I scream out in despair. I can no longer hold it in. I begin to cry. I can't stop it. I don't want to stop it. My whole body heaves up and down between sobs, my breath uneven and short. I think I see Marion return, but my vision is too blurred by the river of tears streaming from my eyes.

I think she's rubbing something on Pax's back. I hear his screams soften to small pathetic whimpers.

"Hush child; this will heal you. Shhhh," Marion gently coaxes.

It starts to sink in that Pax is no longer screaming, which allows me to slow my tears. I choke back the last few sobs and before I know it, Derek is using his shirt to wipe the liquid from my puffy face.

Still applying the goo to Pax's back, Marion says, "After I was healed enough, I came back to wait for you. I figured you would show up sooner or later. Although I must say I was hoping for a more pleasant reunion."

"Is he…is he going to be alright? He was hit with a fireball. Cici did it," I explain.

"Oh no, he wasn't hit. If the fire had actually touched him, he wouldn't have survived. It got close, yes – close enough to burn. But he'll heal from these wounds. The fact that he can feel the pain is good. It means he still has nerves to feel."

This doesn't comfort me much. I can't feel good about Pax being in so much pain.

"Kenlin's out there fighting Cici and the East at this very moment," I say, starting to sob again.

"Don't you worry about Kenlin, he's been at this for quite a long time and he won't be defeated by a little girl spewing fire."

"But, Marion, there's more," I say letting my tears flow, as the image of Elda's skeletal body creeps inside my head. "There were so many of them…the Bravura. They were chained – barely alive. The East has them! I saw it with my own eyes. I tried to save Elda, but I couldn't. I left her there!" I cry out.

"What? Who's Elda? Where were you?"

"Beyond the skull at Mt. Gracon…it was like…like the East is using them to harvest aether. Elda's one of the Bravura. She's been calling for my help this whole time, but I couldn't get her out! The wizard guarding them is so strong. I didn't know what to do."

"Oh my…oh no," Marion says looking down at the ground, beginning to pace. "This can't be. It can't be happening. Not again." She stops pacing and looks up at me, "Hold on. How'd you get away?"

"Something happened with my talisman. It caused some sort of explosion. I'm not sure how. I just ran and grabbed Pax and Derek to get them home."

"Your talisman? How strange. I thought it was just a trinket," she says to herself. Then she takes both of her bandaged hands and places them on my shoulders, directing my attention on her, "You did the right thing, Arden. You couldn't have freed those Bravura on your own. If there's a wizard guarding them like you say, then you can bet that he's a powerful wizard. You're lucky that you escaped and were able to save your brother and Derek. As soon as we're back in our realm, we'll find a way to get them out," she says trying to console me.

"But we have to go back now. I have to go back for Elda."

"No, now is not the time. We will go back for them, but we have to take care of things here first. It's not safe for us to continue living in this realm, but we're going to have to go back to the house for another night. Pax's wounds will take at least another day to heal before he's well enough to travel," she says, pausing to take a breath. "There's also one last thing that I need you to do before we leave for good."

"What's that?" I ask, fearful of what's coming next.

"I need you to go to school."

CHAPTER 24

Promises

"What? Are you for real, Marion? I think the time for high school has passed," I say.

"Well, not quite. I need you to go to school and tell them that you're moving. Say that you're transferring somewhere else. We have to tie up this one last loose end so they don't think they have a missing person's case on their hands when you disappear for good. We need to protect the Bravura's ability to use this realm. We owe them that much. I'll take care of Pax's school."

"Derek," Marion says turning to face him, "It should be safe for you to go back home. The Easterners aren't interested in people from this realm and they'll have no reason to come back after we've gone. You'll need to come up with a story to tell your parents. They probably think that you ran away. Just remember to leave out anything about our realm. We can't have them knowing about us – for their safety, as well as yours."

"What about his wounds?" I ask.

She scans his body. His cuts have healed to look more like scratches and all of the bruising and swelling is gone. "I suppose you can just tell them you fell into a thorn bush," she suggests.

"If they already think that I've run away," Derek begins hesitantly, "...do you think I could just write them a letter saying that I've gone travelling abroad or something, so that I can go back with you guys?" he finishes, shooting me a hopeful glance.

Marion sighs, "I'm sorry, Derek, but this is your home. You belong here. If we take you back with us, you'll eventually die. Arden, Pax, and I can only live here a little while before we too have to return to our realm. It's just the way it is. I know we're all going to miss you terribly, but your family and home are here."

"No!" I find myself shouting out of nowhere. "No! There has to be a way. It's not fair. I need him!"

Derek places one of his strong arms around my shoulders and draws me closer to him. "Don't worry, AJ. It's going to be alright. We'll be together somehow. You can't stop what's meant to be. Let's just do what we gotta do and we'll figure everything out later. OK?"

"OK," I respond like a little child, choosing to believe what he says even though I know the truth.

"Now, let's get Pax back to the house. We're going to have to move him very carefully and be certain not to touch his back," Marion instructs.

All three of us gently place our hands under his body. I try not to look at his blistered back, which began oozing a clear liquid after

Marion covered him in her miracle goo. Pax moans as we carry him through the forest back to our house, but his pain has lessened.

As we take our first steps out of the forest, I'm shocked to see what's become of our home. A quarter of the house has been melted away, leaving a covering of ash. The surrounding grass, bushes, the driveway, and what is left of the house are all a miserable grey color, polluted with soot and sadness, like a depressing memorial of our run-in with the East. Almost nothing remains of my bedroom, or Pax's room for that matter. We're forced to lay him on a couch in the basement, which escaped destruction.

Derek and I leave Marion to tend to Pax's wounds and go upstairs to discuss our plan for the day ahead. We have a little time before we have to head to school, so we take a moment and sit together in the grey darkness of the house, silently holding hands. I lean my head on his shoulder and close my eyes, trying to capture this moment in my memory.

"AJ," Derek says, breaking the silence. "I don't care about what happened before. You know I'd take a thousand beatings if it meant more time with you," he says, pausing to let the meaning of his words resonate.

Now it's my turn to comfort him. I slowly kiss the scratches that are left on his hands and arms as if my kisses are magic kisses that will make them go away for good. Then I take my fingers and brush the hair on his forehead to the side. I look deep into his blue eyes and kiss him on the lips with all of my being.

"This isn't the end, AJ. I promise," he says after our lips part.

"Let's just focus on what we need to do, right?" I say, reminding him of his own words.

He takes his hand and interlocks his fingers in mine. His eyes scan my face. "There's something else on your mind. I can tell."

"It's just that I can't stop thinking about Elda and all of those Bravura. I have this image of them in my head. All chained up. They need me, but I don't know how to help them. I don't know how to get them out of there."

"You'll figure it out, AJ. You got me out of that prison didn't you? I know you and you're strong. You'll go back to your world and you'll find a way to rescue them. Elda was speaking to you for a reason, right?"

"I guess. She said that I have the power to free them."

"Then you do. I know you do."

He always knows the right thing to say. Always. I feel so much stronger with him around. How am I supposed to cope when he's no longer there?

He kisses me on the hand and we reluctantly move away from each other. It's time to come back to reality. Derek heads to his house to face the wrath of his parents, while I look over the remains of my former home. An unexpected joy fills my heart when Sasha comes pouncing forward, knocking me backwards. I don't know how long Marion has been back, but Sasha looks like someone has been taking care of her.

"Hey girl," I say, scratching her behind the ears. "Go find Paxy."

She obediently sniffs him out and joins him in the basement.

There's nothing left of my clothes, so I have to call Emily and ask her to bring an extra uniform to school for me.

"Arden! Oh my goodness – I thought you were dead or something!"

"No, I'm fine. My clothes got the worst of it. Mind bringing me a spare uniform?"

"Oh no – your clothes? That's *terrible*! We'll have to go shopping!"

"Sure, sounds good. See you in a bit."

I don't have the heart to tell her that we won't ever get the chance to go shopping. I pull out an old t-shirt and pair of jeans that were stored away in a box in the basement and put them on. They smell like a mixture of basement and ash, but it's the best I can do considering the circumstances.

Walking over to Derek's this morning feels strange. I know it's the last time I'll be doing this and it adds a sense of finality to the moment. Like our time together was just a passing phase in our lives and now we have to move on. We're silent on the way to school. The significance of the day ahead is occupying my thoughts. I stare out the window in a daze. The scenery has somehow taken on a different look. Everything seems more… precious. The leaves on the trees have turned gorgeous jewel tones and the picturesque mountains set against the flawlessly blue sky make the whole scene heartbreakingly beautiful. Even the school appears changed – not so threatening.

I see the crowds of kids flowing by, but it's like I'm watching them from another plane – here, but not fully here. All of my old cares no longer concern me and I can see these people for what they really are. Just kids trying to find their way through life. They're not the real danger. There are far worse things to face.

I get out of the Honda and shut its rusty door. Emily bounces up to me and hands me one of her spare uniforms. It's much too small, but I think I can squeeze myself into it.

"Arden! I'm so glad you're back!" she exclaims, hugging me exuberantly. "Everyone thought something crazy was going on! First you disappeared, then Derek. And then Zeke and Cici. I didn't know *what* to think! You should hear what people are saying! The best is the one where you all had to flee to Mexico to escape the Feds!"

"Wow. Fleeing to Mexico? Someone has an overactive imagination," I say dryly.

"The truth is way less exciting," Derek chimes in. "Me and Arden were sick with mono."

"Mono?" Emily asks, her eyes lighting up. "Like as in the kissing disease?"

"Yup. That's the one," Derek says, trying to hide his smirk.

"You had to go with mono?" I whisper to Derek, annoyed at his choice of alibis.

"Now everybody knows I kissed the most beautiful girl in school," he explains with a devilish grin.

"What happened to Zeke and Cici?" Emily ponders aloud.

"Maybe they have mono too," I reply, laying on the sarcasm.

"Ew! Gross!" She exclaims before turning and running off to class.

"Jeez, it was only a joke," I say, laughing a little.

This reminds me that today, there'll be no Zeke and Cici. This thought should bring me some comfort, but it doesn't. Soon I'll be returning to a world filled with thousands of Easterners just like them.

Derek gives me a hug before going to class, but instead of going to first period, I head to the front office. With reluctance, I push open the heavy glass doors and step inside. The secretary, Velma, is an older woman with kind eyes. I've spent many an hour sitting in this office on my way to see the Principal and she's always been a good sport about it. She smiles when she sees me.

"Why such a gloomy guss?" she asks in her old raspy voice.

"Well Velms, it looks like today is the day that you and I say goodbye. My family's moving," I reply.

"That's good, right? I thought you didn't like it here," she says with a little glint in her eye.

"I don't…it's just… well I hate goodbyes." *And now I'll be fighting for the rest of my life in a vicious war taking place in another realm.*

"Don't we all," she responds and starts getting my paperwork together.

I spend the rest of the day saying my farewells – first to Emily. She immediately starts crying. Through her tears, she tells me about the big plans she had to make me over so I would finally know what it's like to be cute. I thank her for her thoughtfulness and assure her that I'll work on my cuteness even in her absence. After that, I make sure to see a few key teachers and thank them for putting up with me during the last few years.

The next thing I know, I find myself mindlessly drifting towards the benches out back.

He's already there waiting for me.

"I was counting on you showing up," Derek says.

"Yeah, I guess I can't leave without paying my respects." I take a seat next to him.

After a moment or so of silence he says, "What do you think is going happen to you when you go back?"

"I don't know. I was in training before, maybe they'll send me back there. I just want to save the Bravura. And I want to be with my family."

"This must've been really hard for you, AJ. Just remember that you have someone here who cares about you. I'm your family too."

"There's no way I could ever forget you, Derek."

"I don't care what happened before. I want to remember everything," he says to me. "I need to. No matter how painful it is."

I couldn't agree with him more. There's not a single moment I would give up. Even the ones that hurt. These are *our* memories, and they're all I'm going to have left of him.

Since I've finished all of my goodbyes and I have my alibi nicely set-up, Derek and I decide to ditch the rest of school and head home. I'm anxious to see how Pax is doing and truth-be-told, I just can't take any more. I wasn't built to handle this much emotion in one day.

Back at home we find that Pax is recovering well. His back is freshly pink, like new skin has formed where the blisters were. Marion's busy wrapping him in gauze since his skin is still very sensitive. The only shirt Pax can manage to keep on without being too bothered is one of Kenlin's enormously large old, lightweight t-shirts. It's good to see him looking so well, and he and Sasha are back to being buddies. She doesn't leave his side.

I start thinking about how bad it's going to be for Pax to have to say goodbye to Sasha, and Marion seems to read my thoughts.

"Don't worry, Arden. All the animals will be going back with us."

"Well at least there's that," I respond, my voice sounding more sullen than I had intended.

Pax is well enough to move around, so Marion decides that it's best for us to leave soon. We don't want to take any chances by staying here too long. All four of us make our way outside to the back of the house.

"Ok honey, time to say your last goodbye. We'll meet you in the forest," Marion says to me.

Marion and Pax leave me and Derek to go ready the horses. We're alone for the last time.

I'm too upset to speak. What can I say that I haven't already? He knows that I would change things if I could. That I want more than anything to be with him. I use my arms wrapped around his body and my kisses to do my talking for me.

"I'll be here waiting for you, AJ. You know that, right? I'm not going anywhere, no matter how long it takes," he says between kisses.

The funny thing is that I believe him. I know that he'll wait for me. Because I'll be waiting for him too. It's not a choice. It's a necessity. We need each other.

"I'll find a way. Even if it means altering the rules of the universe," I say with a sad laugh.

I turn to leave him, standing alone, watching me walk into the forest to face my new life. Both of us know that things will never be the same. But maybe that's OK.

"Wait!" he yells.

I turn back to look at him one last time while I walk away.

"I love you, AJ," he shouts as the distance between us visibly grows.

CHAPTER 25

Going Home

The sight of the five of them – Pax, Marion, Gala, Nalda, and Sasha – all waiting for me at the old oak tree, is reassuring. At least I won't be going back by myself this time.

"Where are we headed?" I ask Marion. "It's probably not safe to go directly back to Mt. Gracon."

"No, we'll need to enlist some help before heading back there. We should find your parents first."

"But I don't have the slightest idea where to begin looking for them. My dad's shop was attacked by the East and I'm not even sure he made it out."

"Oh dear. If he's been captured…" she says, and draws in a big breath. "Don't worry, I know where to go. It's a secret place. If your father escaped the East, there's a good chance he'll be there."

"That's a pretty big *if*."

"We'll know soon enough. I'm not a betting woman, but if I was, I'd bet all my money on your father making it out."

"How are we getting there?" Pax asks.

"This spot here, by this old oak tree, is a node. With enough concentration, I can take us there," Marion says.

I take one final look back towards my old house. We're too deep into the forest to see it, but I picture it in my mind the way it used to be before the fire, before the chaos that changed my life forever. I know this place is no longer my home, but it'll always be a part of me. Nothing can ever change that.

I turn back to face the others. Marion is a little rusty with her transporting skills. We stand huddled together like a very odd rugby team for about five minutes. My talisman heats up as we stand there until we're eventually pulled away. When we reappear, we land at the edge of a large lake. Gala and Nalda are frightened of the water and neigh loudly before trotting away to safety. Sasha; however, happily pads along the edge of the lake where the water meets the earth, leaving little paw prints behind her in the dirt.

Surrounding the lake, about two hundred yards from the edge, are dozens of towering pine trees that look as though they're protecting the water from would-be intruders. The evening sun is low on the horizon and its light reflects softly off the rippling water. Except for the noise the six of us are making, it's eerily silent.

"This is just as I remember it," Marion says, and begins walking towards the water. She walks along the edge, scanning the lake.

I'm half expecting to see the Lochness Monster pop out when I hear her exclaim, "Yes! This is it! Come here children!" After motioning for us to come towards her, she bends down low to the ground and heaves a large, moss-covered rock to the side.

Pax and I guide our two very disinclined horses towards Marion, while Sasha enthusiastically tromps forward. Before I have time to yell "STOP," our faithful pup continues right on into the water, disappearing from sight.

"Sasha! No!" Pax yells.

"Quiet, Pax, you mustn't draw attention!" Marion scolds. "Now take Sasha's lead and follow her in."

"You want us to go down there... into the water?" I ask.

"Yes, that's exactly what I want you to do. Now move it! You go in first and I'll make sure the horses are set up," Marion says.

"They aren't coming?"

"No, they're much too big to go down there. They'll be fine out here. Trust me, they won't go too far," she says, before removing their bridles and releasing them.

I venture towards the water first, Pax following behind me. As I step towards the spot where Sasha disappeared, I see that there's a place beneath the edge of the lake where the water stops and a downwards slope begins. The hole is just large enough to fit a person through. I plunge downwards, feet first, before I notice the bars built into one side of the cavity. It's too late to grab ahold of them, and I continue sliding until I crash into a soft dirt mound.

Pax is more observant and uses the bars to guide himself down with ease.

"Going for a short-cut?" Pax teases.

"Ha ha," I say rubbing the dirt from my back.

Marion begins to lower herself down after Pax, but before coming all the way, she stops and drags the mossy rock over the top of the hole. It takes a few attempts and a lot of huffing and puffing before she's able to get it in the right spot.

Small torches line the walls of the cramped corridor, providing a dim glowing light.

We move forward down the corridor, which at its end, empties into a large oval-shaped room lined with flat, smooth stones. Inside the room, there are several beds pushed up against the wall. In the center, a family is sitting down at an oversized, wooden table to have dinner – my family.

I was beginning to think that this day would never come and she almost doesn't seem real to me. I would pinch myself, but I'm too shocked to move.

"Mom?" I say.

"Arden! Pax!" she shouts and bolts from the table, throwing her arms around us. "Oh my darlings, I'm so happy you're alright!" Pax yelps a little from the sudden touch on his back.

She pulls away to look us over. My mother is more stunning than I could've imagined. Her face resembles mine, but holds an

intense, authentic beauty I haven't seen before. She has a savage kind of exquisiteness to her.

"Is that really you?" I ask.

"Yes, it's me," she says laughing and crying at the same time.

Pax begins to cry and my mother pulls his face in closer to hers until their foreheads touch. They stand there crying together and I can't bring myself to look away. The next thing I know, my father has one arm wrapped around the other side of Pax. Everyone is here. Everyone is OK. I almost don't believe it yet, but as we stand there a feeling of wholeness runs through me, filling the tiny cavities in my heart that I didn't even know existed.

When we finally part, I see that my father's arm is in a sling.

"What happened to you? Are you OK?" I ask him.

"Oh this is nothing. Just a sprain," he replies. "You might say I got a little too enthusiastic when the East attacked my shop. The heat of the moment, you know."

"Sometimes your father forgets that creating weapons is his specialty, not using them," my mother says with a light laugh, wiping away the remainder of her tears.

We make our way to the table. Kenlin and Dannia are there waiting for us. Besides some scrapes and bruises, everyone looks alright. We sit down to eat, as if we're just a normal family having dinner after a long day. Only, the topic of conversation isn't what I would call normal.

"I'm sorry that we couldn't reach you sooner, Arden. You've probably figured out the message you got at camp was a trick," Dannia says.

"Yeah, we caught on a little late," I reply, remembering my father's ruined apothecary shop. "What happened to you guys? By the time we got to the shop you were gone."

"The East attacked while I was there, but I don't think they were expecting me," she continues. "Father and I fought them off and escaped."

"We went in search of your mother. For all we knew, she may have been in danger too," my dad says. "We thought you were safe at camp and didn't know about the message until Marcus was able to reach us much later."

"Did they hurt you, Pax?" Dannia asks hesitantly. "Kenlin told us what happened."

"Nah, I'm OK."

Dannia moves closer to Pax, studying his face. "You look different from the last time I saw you. You're so big. I can't believe you're my baby brother."

Pax blushes a bit now that everyone is staring at him.

Turning the attention away from himself, he says, "Sorry for leaving you like that, Kenlin."

"Don't worry. I wanted you to escape. Besides, after you left, there wasn't much fighting to be done. Cici went into quite a rage

when she saw you disappear and lit such a large fire that my men and I were able to hide in the smoke and get away."

"Kenlin," I interrupt. "Did you see them? All of those Bravura? The East has them. We have to figure out some way to get them out."

"Yes, I saw them," Kenlin replies.

"We've already alerted the leaders of the Western Kingdoms," my mom assures me. "They're planning an attack on Mt. Gracon as we speak."

"We have to get them out of there. I promised one of the Bravura, Elda. She's counting on me. They all are."

"You spoke to them?" my mom asks.

"Yes, Elda had been sending me messages, but I didn't realize what they were. I barely made it out of there myself. If it wasn't for my talisman, I may not be here."

"Your talisman?" my father interjects. "What about it? Did you use it?"

"I think so, I think it was drawing in the aether, but I don't know how. It caused an explosion and I escaped."

"So it works! I knew it would work! This means that it's been activated."

"Perhaps now's not the time to be so excited," my mom says, putting her hand on his shoulder.

"You don't understand. I worked on it for so long, but I never had the chance to test it. Now that I know that it works, we have a real shot at fighting back!" he says with wide eyes. "But we'll have to act quickly. From what Kenlin described, it seems that the East has built a contraption that stores the aether the Bravura are gathering. They're using the Bravura to pull the aether from the node, willing the magic out of its hiding place in the atmosphere and forcing it into the spheres. I haven't seen anything like it – it could shift the whole dynamic of the war. Their power will be limitless if we don't put an end to it."

"You said Elda was sending you messages?" Dannia asks.

"Yeah, Elda was showing me where she was in my dreams – a glimpse into the future. I didn't realize it until we were there. Maybe I was supposed to change the future. I was too blind. I didn't change anything. They're still there in chains. I've failed them," I say, on the verge of tears.

"It's not your fault you didn't know what the dream meant," my mother says. "You're just beginning to understand your abilities. The important thing is that their message was received and now that we know of them, the West *will* save them."

"Yes, and remember, if not for your actions in the prison, your brother and friends might not be alive," Kenlin says. "You didn't fail anyone."

"Just don't try saving anyone like that again, OK?" my mom says, brushing my ponytail from my shoulder.

"Hopefully, you'll never need to use your heart chamber in that manner again. I have a plan and I think now is the time to act," my father says. "Pax," he says turning to my brother, "You and Arden will go to the Bravura training camp and work on developing your skills. We need you both to be at your strongest."

"What do you need us to do?" Pax asks.

"For now, I just need you to train. I can't tell you anymore," my father replies.

"Don't worry, Pax. I'll help you through training," Dannia says.

I raise one eyebrow at my sister, remembering what her idea of "helping" is.

Marion and Kenlin, now free to go after having fulfilled their duties as our guardians, decide they would rather stay and help with my father's plan against the East.

"I'm not just going to let you two run amok after all the hard work I've put into making you decent," Marion says.

We spend the next several hours sitting around the table talking. My mother tells us about her adventures in battle and what it was like to be raised by a Chief. I find out that Dannia has a boyfriend who's off fighting in the war right now. They've been dating for two years. Pax and Kenlin share their hunting stories, and I can see how proud my mother is that Pax has inherited her natural Hebelcaan abilities. When I can no longer keep my eyes open, I make my way to one of the beds and collapse into a deep slumber.

I find myself in a beautiful green meadow, filled with bright yellow and white flowers. The sun is shining and tiny butterflies flit from flower to flower. I'm the happiest I've ever been. I walk through the meadow, letting my fingers brush the tops of the flowers as I pass by and raise my face to the sun to take in all of its warmth. I finally feel the peace inside I've been craving for so long.

Then a shadow crosses my eyelids, blocking the sun's rays and causing me to open my eyes. It's suddenly dark, and I hear a rustling from the other side of the meadow.

"It's coming," says a low, but distinct male voice.

I know this voice.

"You must prepare," the voice whispers urgently, as if it is frightened.

"Zeke?" I whisper back.

I awake to a burning in my chest.

www.ingramcontent.com/pod-product-compliance
Lightning Source LLC
Chambersburg PA
CBHW070601130626

46556CB00001B/235